Uh-oh.

I saw two flashes go past and the coyote brothers were out of there. I mean, you'd have thought they'd been shot out of a cannon. All at once *they were gone.*

But what was the deal? What had caused them to leave out in such a hurry? I edged my way over to the barrel and peered inside. At first I saw nothing in the gloomy darkness. Then I heard the rattle of some paper and in the darky gloomness I began to see . . .

You won't believe this.

I promise you won't.

It was one of the scariest things I'd seen in my whole career.

It was a Garbage Monster from Outer Space!

r

The Garbage Monster from Outer Space

The Garbage Monster
from Outer Space

John R. Erickson

Illustrations by Gerald L. Holmes

Puffin Books

PUFFIN BOOKS
Published by the Penguin Group
Penguin Putnam Books for Young Readers,
345 Hudson Street, New York, New York 10014, U.S.A.
Penguin Books Ltd,
27 Wrights Lane, London W8 5TZ, England
Penguin Books Australia Ltd,
Ringwood, Victoria, Australia
Penguin Books Canada Ltd,
10 Alcorn Avenue, Toronto, Ontario, Canada M4V 3B2
Penguin Books (N.Z.) Ltd,
182-190 Wairau Road, Auckland 10, New Zealand

Penguin Books Ltd, Registered Offices:
Harmondsworth, Middlesex, England

First published in the United States of America simultaneously
by Viking Children's Books and Puffin Books, members of
Penguin Putnam Books for Young Readers, 1999

3 5 7 9 10 8 6 4

LIBRARY OF CONGRESS CATALOGING-IN-PUBLICATION DATA
Erickson, John R.
The garbage monster from outer space / John R. Erickson ;
illustrations by Gerald L. Holmes.
p. cm. — (Hank the Cowdog ; 32)
Summary: Hank the Cowdog is determined to find out who's behind
the series of garbage barrel raids for which he is being held responsible.
ISBN 0-670-88488-X (Viking : hc). — ISBN 0-14-130422-7 (Puffin : pb)
[1. Dogs—Fiction. 2. West (U.S.)—Fiction. 3. Humorous stories.
4. Mystery and detective stories.] I. Holmes, Gerald L., ill. II. Title.
III. Series: Erickson, John R. Hank the Cowdog ; 32.
PZ7.E72556Gar 1999 [Fic]—dc21 98-41784 CIP AC

Hank the Cowdog® is a registered trademark of John R. Erickson.

Printed in the United States of America

CONTENTS

CHAPTER ONE

Prowlers
in the Night

It's me again, Hank the Cowdog. It all began innocently enough. Never in my wildest dreams would I have supposed that I would run away from the ranch, join up with a band of wild cannibals, and then be attacked by a Garbage Monster from Outer Space.

Pretty heavy-duty stuff, huh? You bet it was. A lot of dogs couldn't have handled all that adventure, and a lot of dogs would have been scared to death by an invasion of Garbage Monsters from Outer Space. For me, it was just another job on the ranch.

Have I mentioned that I'm Head of Ranch Security? I am, and it's a very dangerous job. When monsters from outer space land, I'm the one who gets the call.

Anyways, it must have been around 0600 on the morning of September the something. The fourteenth or fifteenth, I guess. It was still pitch-black outside and the air had the smell of fall. Drover and I had spent most of the night doing Sweeps and Patrols of headquarters.

We were exhausted. Who wouldn't have been exhausted? We had checked out the machine shed, the chicken house, the corrals, and the saddle shed. We had routed a couple of Night Monsters out of those bushes near the cellar and barked a reply to a bunch of noisy coyotes.

Drover was ready to call it quits. So was I. We'd done our job. We'd brought the ranch through another dangerous night and it was time to warm up our gunnysacks. We fluffed up our sacks and collapsed. Within seconds, we were both . . . I almost said "sound asleep," but at that very moment, I heard a sound.

Was that some kind of clue? Think about it. "Sound" and "sound asleep." Maybe not, but the point is that just as I was standing on the diving board of life, preparing to go soaring into the swimming pool of . . . something . . . sleep, I sup- pose . . . just as I was so-forthing, I heard an odd sound.

Clunk.

I responded at once. I lifted one Earascope and used it to probe the darkness for other soundatory patterns. Sure enough, there were more sounds: scratching, rattling, and rustling sounds. Something was going on out there, and even though we were worn out and exhausted, we had to respond. After all, we were the elite troops of the Security Division, the ranch's first line of defense against . . . well, you name it. Anything and everything.

"Drover, I've just picked up some strange signals on E-scope. You'd better go check it out."

I heard new odd sounds, these coming from Drover: "Mork snirk buzz bumble."

"Drover, wake up. You've been chosen for an important mission. Congratulations and wake up." No answer, just more incoherent grunts and wheezes. "Drover, I'll give you a count of three to wake up. One. Two. Porkchop sizzle pizzle buzz-bomb murgle."

Okay, maybe I dozed off in the middle of the . . . hey, who wouldn't have dozed off? I was exhausted, wiped out, worn down to a nubbin from all the cares and worries of protecting the ranch. But it was a short doze. I was jerked from the warm vapors of sleep. E-scope was picking up more signals out there in the darkness.

Clunk. Scratch. Rustle. Rattle.

Okay, that did it. I hit the Exit Sleep button and kicked all the Wake-up Circuits over into Data Control's master program. I jacked myself up to a sitting position and ... well, yawned. That's what we do when we've been yanked out of a peaceful sleep. It's very important. It loosens up the jaw muscles and the tongue muscles, and it also rushes fresh air into the body cavity.

I yawned and then beamed a hot glare at my sleeping assistant. "Drover, wake up." Nothing but grunting and wheezing. I would have to go to sterner measures. "Drover? Scrap Time!"

Now get this. His head shot up and he leaped to his feet and began staggering around in a circle. "Scraps! Oh my gosh, it's dark, I'm blind! Hank, help, I can't see, and somebody stole one of my legs!"

"Easy, son. You're not blind."

"Then how come I can't see anything?"

"It's still dark. I haven't barked up the sun yet."

"Oh my gosh, what day is it? Who's on first? Where's my leg?"

Waking up Drover was always an interesting experience. "Your leg is just where you left it, and so is the day. Just relax."

"Oh, okay." He collapsed into a heap, I mean, went down like a rock.

"Hey, get up. You've got work to do. Get out of

that bed or I'll have to growl you out."

He staggered to his feet again. "No, don't do that, you know I can't stand criticism in the morning." He blinked his eyes and looked around. "Gosh, it's dark. I thought you said it was Scrap Time. You lied."

"I did not lie, Drover. I told a small fib to wake you up. There's a huge difference between a fib and a lie."

"Like what?"

"A fib is a small lie for your own good."

"What's so good about it?"

"You've been chosen, out of all the dogs on the ranch, to lead an important mission. I didn't want you to miss out on this great opportunity. Congratulations."

"Gosh, thanks." He yawned.

"Don't yawn when I'm talking to you. It's impolite and disrespectful."

"But I just woke up."

"That's no excuse. There's a time to yawn and there's a time to un-yawn."

"I ate an onion once. Made me sick as a dog."

"Well, what did you expect? If you're a dog, Drover, you can't very well be sick as a horse. Had you ever thought of that?"

"Not really."

"So there you are. It all fits together." There was a moment of silence. I thought I heard him yawn again. "Did you just yawn?"

"No, that wasn't me."

"Good. What were we discussing? I seem to have lost my train of thought."

"Onions."

"Yes, of course. Drover, you should never eat an onion. It will make you as sick as a horse, but that's not what we were talking about."

"We'd just decided to go back to bed."

"Exactly. Well, good night, Drover, I hope you get a good . . . wait a minute. I just woke you up."

"Yeah. I fibbed, but it was for my own good. You said that was okay."

I stuck my nose in his face and gave him a growl. "Listen, you tuna, I woke you up for a very important reason. I picked up signals on E-scope. I want you to check it out. Do you have any problem with that?"

"Yeah. What's an E-scope?"

"Ears, Drover. Earatory Scanners. Earascopes."

"That's three names. I only have two ears."

"If you keep blabbering and wasting my valuable time, you might end up with only one ear. Now get out there and see what was causing those odd sounds."

He walked around in circles. "Which way? I don't know where to go, and boy, this old leg is . . ."

"Over there, Drover, toward the garbage barrels. I'll stay here and defend Command Central. We'll maintain constant radio contact. Oh, and your code name for this mission is Flaming Pretzel."

He burst out with a silly giggle. "Tee-hee, that's funny—Flaming Pretzel."

"It's not funny at all, Drover. It's not only very serious, it's also Top Secret. Do you realize that we're the only dogs in the world who know the true meaning of Flaming Pretzel?"

"Yeah, and even I don't know what it means."

"Exactly, and neither do I. That gives you some idea of just how secret and important this mission is. Even those of us who will carry out the mission can't be trusted with its true meaning. Congratulations, Drover. Now get on with it. Good hunting."

With much whimpering and whining, he set out on his mission. Once he was gone, I . . . heh, heh . . . did a quick spin around my gunnysack and flopped down. See, I had done some calculations and figured that I could grab ten minutes of sack time before I had to bark up the sun. When you're Head of Ranch Security, you grab your sleep when it's grabbable, because when it's not grabbable, it's . . . snork murk borgle muff . . .

Perhaps I dozed. Yes, I'm sure I did, but I was soon dragged from my slumbers by the crackling of the radio.

"Hank, this is . . . I forgot my name, over."

"Pork Chop."

"Okay. Hank, this is Flaming Pork Chop, over, and I've found something out here, over and over. You'd better come check it out, over and over and over."

Huh? Over and over and over? Who was . . . what the . . . oh, yes, it was Drover. Do you get the secret meaning? *Over + Dr = Drover.*

I shook the sleep out of my vapors. "This is Command Central to Flagrant Pretzel. Come back on that last repeat. Report. Repeat the report."

"I've found something out here and it looks pretty serious. You'd better come see, over and under."

I heaved a sigh and pushed myself up on all fours. Well, my sleep was finished and duty was calling. I yawned. We always yawn first thing . . . I've already said that. I yawned and stretched and rolled the muscles in my enormous shoulders, and lumbered out into the predawn darkness to find my nincompoop assistant.

Chances were that he had found nothing at all, or maybe a stray cricket, but I had to check it out. That was my job, after all, and when you're Head of Ranch Security, the bug stops here. Within seconds, I had located Drover's position.

He was crouched behind a chinaberry tree. "Okay, what seems to be the problem?"

"Well, let me think here. I saw three garbage barrels."

"Yes, that checks out. Those are Sally May's garbage barrels. She puts garbage in them and burns it once a week. What's the point?"

"Well, there's no garbage in them."

"Hmm. That's odd. How do you explain that?"

"Well, it's scattered all over the ground."

"Hmmm. That's even odder. Sally May isn't the kind of woman who throws her garbage on the ground. I don't like the sound of this, Drover. Could it be that she's undergone a complete change of personality?"

"Yeah, either that or those five coons tipped over the barrels and scattered the garbage."

HUH? Five coons?

And so it was that the mystery began, a mystery that would soon lead me into deadly combat with a clan of coons, and would end with me being . . .

You'll see.

I Tear Down a Whole Tree and Thrash Several Coons

I peered into the darkness and studied the situation. Much to my amazement, Drover had not only given a fairly accurate description of the problem, but he had even come up with the correct number of coons. There were five of them, and fellers, they were making a mess of things.

They're experts at making messes, don't you know. They're never content just to take what they need and leave. Oh no. They find some kind of fiendish pleasure in wrecking things, whether it's a corn patch, a chicken house, or a garbage barrel. Or three garbage barrels.

I watched them and felt a growing sense of out-

rage. My master's wife had spent a lot of hours and a lot of days trying to make the place look nice and presentable. Now, here were these bandits, these raccoon thugs, making a mockery of all her hard work. The longer I watched, the madder I got.

"Drover, are you going to sit there watching this outrage, or will you do something to teach those villains a lesson?"

"Oh . . . probably just sit here. How about you?"

"Are you suggesting that I might be afraid to go into combat against five coons?"

"Well . . . it makes sense to me."

"Yes, it does, doesn't it? I mean, combat against one coon is dangerous enough, but five . . . a guy could sure get his face plowed."

"Yeah, and I'm still worried about this old leg. The pain got worse when I saw the coons. I think I've got an allergy to coons."

I beamed him a stern glare. "You've got an allergy to life, Drover. I think you're afraid of your own shadow."

"How'd you know that?"

"Just a wild guess."

"Yeah, I saw it last evening and it gave me a terrible scare. It was ten feet long and I thought it was a monster without a tail. But I didn't want anybody to know. You won't tell, will you?"

"Nobody would believe it, Drover. And do you know what else I can't believe?"

"The tooth fairy?"

"No."

"The Easter Bunny?"

"No."

"Bone monsters?"

"If you'll hush, I'll tell you."

"Well, you asked."

"I'm sorry I asked. I can't believe that we've got such a chicken liver in the Security Division. It's disgraceful."

"Well . . . you said you were scared of coons."

"I did not say that. I said that five coons were a lot of coons."

"Yeah, but not as many as six."

"What is your point, Drover? Are you trying to say that I'm just as much of a scaredy-cat as you?"

"Well . . . if you were, I'd feel better."

I pushed myself up to a standing position. "Well, you can forget that. Do you know what I'm fixing to do? I'm going to march into the middle of those coons and give them the thrashing they so richly deserve."

"Oh, how brave!"

"And do you know why? Because you've been an inspiration to me, Drover. You are such a weenie and talking with you is so boring, you've inspired me to do something really crazy, just to get away from you."

"Gosh, thanks, Hank."

"By the sheer force of your lousy example, you've forced me into doing what is good and right. And if you have any pride left in that stub-tailed carcass of yours, you'll follow me into battle to fight for Sally May's garbage barrels."

"In a pig's eye."

"What?"

"I said . . . oh boy, combat. Oh goodie."

"That's better. Now, aren't you proud of being ashamed of yourself?"

"I'm kind of confused right now."

"You'll get over it. Are we ready? She'll be very proud of us, Drover."

"Yeah, or she'll think we did it."

"What? Speak up, son, you're muttering."

"I said . . ."

"Never mind, we're out of time. We must strike while the kettle is black. I'll go in the first wave, you come in the second. Give 'em the full load of barking. If we make enough noise, maybe they'll run. Ready? Oh, and don't forget to yell, 'Freeze, turkey!' That's very important."

"I thought they were coons."

I stared into the vacuum of his eyes. "Are you trying to be funny?"

"No, but you said . . . I thought . . . boy, I sure get confused."

"Never mind, Drover. Just follow orders, and remember that this one is for Sally May."

"Yeah, but if the coons run off and she finds us . . ."

"Silence. Let's move out. Good luck, soldier, and break a leg."

"I've already got one bad leg. It's killing me."

I slipped forward on paws that made not a sound, paws that had been trained for commando work and silent missions and so forth. Twenty yards out, I could see the coons shooting baskets with a bean can, tossing newspapers into the air, spreading ugly garbage for the sheer meanness of it. My sense of outrageous anger was growing by the second. Those guys would pay for this.

Ten yards out, we emerged from the cover of the chinaberry grove, and for the first time, the rioting coons realized that they were surrounded. Ha! You should have seen the shock and surprise on their faces. This would be a piece of cake.

I gave the order to attack and went zooming into the middle of them, yelling "Charge, bonzai!" at the top of my lungs. Drover brought up the Second Wave, and he was yipping and squeaking. Do you know what he was yipping and squeaking? "Frozen turkey, frozen turkey!"

Oh brother. I was tempted to call off the attack and give him a scolding right there on the spot, but there wasn't time. What kind of brain can take the command "Freeze, turkey!"

and turn it into "Frozen turkey"? Drover's brain, and there is nothing more to be said.

And besides, I had five coons to whip.

I went charging right into the middle of them. I could see their faces now. Those guys were ... uh ... growling and humping their backs, as coons often do when they ... and several of those guys were pretty big ... real big and ... good grief, they were coming out after me!

I went to Full Air Brakes on all four paws, slid to a stop, and then executed a quick Reverse Spin. I hit Full Power on all engines, spun my paws in the dirt, slammed into Drover, and kept truckin'.

"Drover, we're going to Plan B!"

"I didn't know we had a Plan B."

"We do now. It's called Total Disarray and Run for Your Life!"

"Oh my leg!"

Yipes, one of the coons jumped me from behind. He was chewing on my ears and the back of my neck. It hurt! I tried to buck, I ran in circles, I leaped into the air. The coon hung on and continued meat-grinding my ears. I saw a tree up ahead. Maybe if I rammed the tree at full speed, it would dislodge my head and neck from the rest of my ... BONK! ... red checkers and fireworks sprayed brilliant colors behind my eyes. I found

myself stumbling around the tree on legs made of
rubber. I became aware of a dull throbbing pain
which seemed to be coming from a lump the size
of a biscuit on the top of my head.

But you know what? It worked, and I mean
worked like a charm. Not only had I shucked off
the coon, but all of them were scampering away
into the morning gloom. What a deal! I mean, sure,
coons tend to disappear at the first light of day,

but the main reason they were fleeing in terror was that they had just seen the Head of Ranch Security ram a huge tree and *break it in half.*

No kidding, broke that tree completely in half, and we're talking about a full-grown chinaberry with a trunk the size of telephone pole. Have I ever mentioned that my name in Coyote Language is "Mump-Wump-Hoosegow"? That means "Dog Who Breaks Trees in Half." Yes siree, and that's why all the coyotes on this outfit RUN when they see me coming.

And so did those ruffian coons. You think they wanted to mess with a dog who tears down trees? Heck no. They ran, fellers, and we're talking about running for their lives.

I sent them packing with a withering barrage of barking. "And let that be a lesson to you, and the next time you mess around with Sally May's garbage barrels, I'll show you some serious tree trashing!"

Pretty impressive, huh? You bet it was. I got 'em told, and then I turned and marched back to the barrels to, well, lay my mark on them and claim them as my own. When Sally May showed up, I wanted her to see, with her very own eyes, that I had recaptured her barrels and returned them to the ranch inventory.

I was in the process of laying a good strong mark on one of the barrels when an odd sound reached my ears. They leaped to Full Alert Position, swiveled around, and homed in on the sound. It was a kind of buzzing noise, and it seemed to be coming from inside one of the . . .

Hmmm, this was strange. A bee perhaps? I abandoned the Mark and Conquer procedure and peed into the barrel . . . *peered* into the barrel, I should say, and one little letter makes quite a difference, doesn't it?

Where was I? Oh yes, the barrel from which the . . . so forth. And there before my very eyes I saw . . . you won't believe what I saw. I couldn't believe it. I was astammered, dumbfoundered.

There, lying on a collection of newspapers and various other items of trash was . . . you probably think it was the Garbage Monster from Outer Space, right? Nope. That comes later in the story. This time, what I discovered was a smallish sleeping raccoon, who was not only small but also asleep.

And you know what else? It was none other than Eddy the Rac.

Pretty amazing, huh? You bet it was.

CHAPTER THREE

Eddy Runs
but I Get Caught

Do you remember Eddy? Quick review. He was an orphan coon, see, that Slim found on the side of the road one day. Slim carried him back to headquarters and raised him in a cage until he was old enough to survive in the wild. We turned him loose when he became such a nuisance and a pain in the neck, nobody could stand him anymore.

Oh, and one more item on Eddy. He was a cheat, a sneak, a hustler, and a con artist—a typical coon, in other words, only even more typical than most. How did I know? It had been my misfortune to be involved in several business deals with him. We don't have time to go into . . .

Oh, what the heck, maybe we have time for one

quick example. Remember his famous Elevator Scam? He was confined to a cage, see, but he wanted out, so what did he do? He called me over and assured me that the cage was actually . . . he told me, on his word of honor, that . . .

This is too embarrassing. I can't go on.

He assured me that the cage was actually an *elevator*. An elevator, and if I stepped inside, I could go for a ride. Can you believe that? I mean, how dumb would you have to be to . . .

The point is—and it makes me sad to report this—the point is that I believed the little sneak, and I'm sorry that I can't report which of us ended up locked in the cage, so just skip it.

Sorry I brought it up.

The funny thing about Eddy was that I kind of liked him. I mean, when he wasn't doing deals and trying to steal the bark off every tree on the ranch, he was a pretty nice guy. And here he was again. He'd been part of the Garbage Barrel Robbery, and all his pals had run off and left him.

And unless someone woke him up and hustled him out of there, he would be discovered by the most dreaded ranch wife in Ochiltree County.

I banged on the side of the barrel. "Hey, you in there, wake up." No response. I banged again, louder this time. "Hey, Eddy, wake up. You need to get out of here before the plot gets any thicker."

No response. Well, that was typical Eddy—play all night and then fall asleep at dawn. I grabbed the scruff of his neck in my enormous jaws and dragged him out. At last he began to stir. One eye slid open. It focused on me, then both eyes popped open. He jumped to his feet, humped his back, and started making those weird sounds coons make when they're cornered.

"Relax, pal, it's just . . ."

BAM!

He slugged me! "Listen, you little malcomgrate, I'm trying to save your hide! It's me, Hank."

He studied me with his beady little eyes. The hump in his back began to . . . whatever the word is. Reseed. Go down. Disappear. Then he spoke. "Oh. Hi. How's it going?"

"Well, for reasons which aren't apparent to me now, I was trying to wake you up and save your skin—for which you punched me in the nose."

"Oh. Yeah. Sorry. Thought you were someone else. Guard dog. Mean, bark, stuff like that."

"Well, I am a guard dog, but in a moment of weakness, I thought I'd save you from a terrible fate. Do you have any idea where you are, pal?"

He glanced around. "Let's see. Job. We pulled

a job, right? Garbage job. With the gang. Where's the gang?"

"They ran, Eddy, and left you sleeping in the barrel."

"Oh yeah. Right. Got sleepy, had to catch a . . . zzzzzzzzz." His head fell on his chest and he was asleep again. With some effort, I managed to bring him around again. "Oh. Hi. Listen, got a deal, me and you."

"Don't talk to me about deals, you little swindler. I've had all of your deals I can stand for one lifetime, and the point is that you'd better get away from here unless you want to get blamed for trashing ranch headquarters. Do you remember Sally May?"

"Yeah. 'When she's angry, the trees run for cover.' Right?"

"Exactly, and if I were you, I'd do that—run for cover. She'll be down here with the morning trash any time now. You'd best head for tall timber and make yourself scarce."

"Right. Thanks. You're a pal." He started backing away. "I'll remember. Look me up sometime. Got a great deal." He turned and monkey-walked into the chinaberry grove.

Well, I had done my good deed for the day and had saved the little sneak from . . . imagine him saying that he had a deal for me! What a laugh. What kind of idiot did he think I was? Hey, I had gone to school on coons and there was no danger of me ever "looking him up" to hear about his so-called "great deal." Ha!

Well, with Eddy gone and out of the way, I returned to the job of marking and reclaiming the ranch garbage barrels. At that point, it suddenly occurred to me that it was time—nay, past time—for me to bark up the sun. Boy, that had been a close call. Just imagine what might have happened if I'd . . .

It was too scary even to think about. The entire earth plunged into darkness. Cowboys groping around for their coffeepots.

You'll be proud and relieved to know that I got 'er done, barked that yellow ball of sun right over the horizon and up into the sky where she belonged. It was about as good a job of as I'd ever done, and at that point I . . .

Hmmmm, became aware, shall we say, of certain fragrant waves that were drifting out of the, uh, plundered garbage barrels. Was it possible that those coons had missed some luscious chicken bones? Yes, the evidence was certainly pointing in that direction. Somewhere inside the second barrel lay a real treasury of . . .

I cast long, probing glances over both shoulders. No one was around. No one was watching. No one would ever know, and what the heck, what could it hurt for me to, uh, salvage a few morsels from a mess that had obviously been caused by coons?

See, my plan all along was to be sitting triumphantly beside the mess when Sally May came down with her morning trash. I wanted her to know who or whom had recaptured the barrels and punished the rioting coons. That would still work. All I had to do was dart inside the barrel, seize the delicious, yummy chicken bones, wolf them down, and then return to my Position of Triumph.

Yes, this would work. I dived into the barrel and began scratching around for . . . I knew they were in there, I mean, the aroma of fried chicken bones was getting really strong and powerful, and all I had to do . . . there was still quite a lot of junk in the bottom and it took some extra-special digging procedures to . . .

"HANK! WHAT ARE YOU . . . GET YOUR-SELF OUT OF THE GARBAGE!"

Huh?

My head snapped up and . . . *clunk* . . . I banged it on the derned barrel, but that was a small concern compared to . . . had I heard a voice? A shrill angry female voice? Gulp. Where had she come from? I mean, I'd checked in all directions and . . . it was too early for her to be . . . I mean, she never brought her trash down at this . . .

I poked my head out. There she was in her bathrobe and slippers. Her hair was . . . how can I say this? She hadn't taken the time to fix her hair for this meeting, shall we say, and it was a wee bit unshoveled. Disheveled. She held a sack of garbage in each arm. Her face was . . . yikes, turning red or purple, and her eyes glowed with an unwholesome light, and her nostrils were beginning to take on the shape of a rattlesnake's head.

Gulp. Those were all signs that she was moving into one of her Thermonuclear Moments.

Our eyes met. I tried to squeeze up a smile, and I heard my tail thumping against the barrel, as it struggled to express my, uh, profound sense of . . .

Her lips moved but no words came out. Then they did. "You . . . you . . . you hound! Look what you've done! I can't believe you'd . . . ohhhh! Scattering trash on your own ranch!"

Boy, that hurt. Her words went through me like a can of worms. She dropped the sacks of trash.

"Well, I'm not going to clean up this wreck, but

I know who *will*. Don't move, I'll be right back."

And with that, she stomped back to the house. The screen door slammed. I heard voices in the house. A moment later, the screen slammed again. Heavy footsteps, several of them, and they were coming in my direction.

I felt terrible about this, just awful, but it occurred to me that I might have just enough time to dart back into the barrel and get those last two or three bones. What the heck, if I was going to take the rap for this deal, I might as well make use of the, uh, salvage rights. I shot back into the depths of the barrel and was in the midst of crunching two lovely drumstick bones when . . . voices? Loud voices?

Uh-oh, maybe I should have skipped those last two bones. Now that I thought about it, a dog didn't appear at his sorrowful best when he was, uh, crunching chicken bones. I crawled out . . . right into the scorching glare of their eyes. She'd brought Loper. And Little Alfred.

"There!" she said, shooting a finger-arrow at my heart. "There's your dog and that is your mess. When you get it all cleaned up—every paper and eggshell—I'll have your breakfast ready."

"Hon, I've got to leave for New Mexico to look at those bulls."

A wicked smile bloomed on her face. "Yes? You'll have to hurry." Just then, we heard Slim's pickup coming down the hill. "Maybe Slim would like to help. You boys have fun." She waved her fingers and returned to the house.

Loper shot a glare at me and seemed on the brink of saying something hateful, but just then Slim came walking up. He had his hands in his pockets and a grin on his mouth.

"Good honk, did the garbage barrels blow up in the night? And who's that layin' in the midst of all the rubble? Why, it's a cute little puppy dog. Huh. Mornin', Loper."

Loper placed a hand on Slim's shoulder. "Slim, old buddy, you know I'd never ask you to do a job that I wouldn't do myself."

"Uh-oh."

"But I've got to be in San Jon, New Mexico, at ten o'clock. If I leave right now, I'll barely make it. We'd hate for me to be late, wouldn't we?"

"I ain't likin' the way this is soundin'."

"And we'd hate for Sally May to have to clean up the mess our dog made, wouldn't we?"

"Our dog?"

"So if you'd volunteer to take care of this business, I'd grab a bite of breakfast and get on the road, and you'd become our Ranch Hero for the Day."

"I've got to haul them cows to the sale barn."

"That'll keep 'til tomorrow. Thanks, pardner." Loper whopped him on the back. "Beneath that lousy personality, you're a warm and wonderful human being. See you tomorrow night."

And with that, Loper hiked up the hill to the house, which left me alone . . . with Alfred and Slim.

Well, I'd been in worse company. Maybe they would understand. We were pals, after all, and they had warm spots in their respective hearts for, uh, dogs and so forth.

Slim beamed me hateful looks, but Alfred came over and put his arm around my neck. And then he whispered, "Hankie, you'd better quit knocking over twash barrels, or my mom's going to find you another home."

Me? Hey, I didn't . . . I was just doing my job, minding my own . . .

What a lousy deal! I had been framed and railroaded and blamed for crimes I didn't commit.

CHAPTER FOUR

I'm Accused
of Terrible Crimes

Now, I'll be the first to admit that being left alone with Slim and Alfred was better than some of the alternatives, but still, this didn't show much promise of being a happy occasion. Slim wasn't thrilled with his assignment. I could tell.

I mean, right away he curled his lip at me and said, "You dufus dog, couldn't you find anything better to do last night?"

I thumped my tail and gave him Hurtful Looks. Wait a minute, I was innocent, perfectly . . . okay, I'd salvaged a couple of measly chicken bones and maybe that hadn't been such a great idea, but . . . coons, it was the coons, and all I'd done was . . .

Nobody wanted to hear my side of the story!

Even Slim, who'd always been a great pal of mine, even Slim had rushed to judgment and convicted me of crimes I didn't commit! Hey, for their information, I had risked my life to defend the ranch against a gang of . . .

"Get out of the barrel, Muttfuzz, unless you want to spend the rest of your life in there—which might not be such a bad idea."

He raised up the garbage barrel and, fine, I could move. And no, I sure didn't want to spend the rest of my life in a trash heap, but the point here, the tragic point, was that nobody was listening to my side of the story.

Why didn't he look down at the ground! The evidence was right there in front of his nose: coon tracks, dozens of them. Did I leave coon tracks? Heck no, but did he bother to look for clues? Had it ever occurred to Loper or Sally May that . . .

What a fool I'd been for helping Eddy the Rac escape! If I'd just left him sleeping in the barrel, he would have been caught lefthanded and charged with the crime. Instead, I had to sit there and listen to Slim gripe and grumble.

And he did plenty of that. Every time he bent over to pick up a piece of rubbish, he shot a glare at me and muttered something under his breath. I didn't catch all of it, but I heard enough to know that I had already been tried and convicted.

So there I was, thinking about all the injustice in the world, when who should show up but my least favorite character on the ranch. Pete the Barncat. I saw him at a distance and hoped he would stay out of my way. Did he? Of course not. Pete is a genius when it comes to showing up at exactly the wrong time.

Have I mentioned that I don't like cats? I don't like cats, and Pete is at the head of the list of Cats I Don't Like.

He was sliding along, see, purring like a little . . . something . . . chain saw, motorboat, refrigerator . . . and rubbing up against everything in sight. Oh, and he was grinning. Why would a cat be grinning at that hour of the morning? I wasn't sure, but I knew that he was up to no good. I tried to ignore him, in hopes he might go away. He didn't. He came up and started rubbing on my legs, and then he grinned up at me and said, "Hi, Hankie," in that simpering, whiny voice of his.

I hate that. It drives me nuts. My ears jumped. My lips rose into a snarl and a growl began to form deep in the missile silo of my throat. "Kitty, I must warn you that I'm having a bad day, and seeing you only makes it worse. You might want to move along."

He continued to rub. "Poor doggie! What seems to be the trouble?"

"I don't discuss my troubles in front of cats. Sorry. We have rules against that."

"Do you really? Then let me guess."

"I'm sorry, but we have rules against cats guessing."

"My goodness, Hankie, you have so many rules."

"That's right, Kitty, and that happens to be one of the major differences between us dogs and you cats. We live by rules. You cats live by nothing but your own selfish desires."

"Oh, I think you have it wrong, Hankie." He batted his eyes and smirked. "Dogs live by rules, but cats just . . . rule."

I glared down at the little pest and tried to think of a scorching reply. I couldn't think of anything really special, so I said, "Pete, that's the dumbest thing you've said since the last dumb thing you said. And stop rubbing on my legs."

"My goodness, Hankie, do you have rules against that too?"

"Yes, as a matter of fact, we do. Rule Twelve in the Cowdog Manual of Conduct states in no uncertain terms that cats 'shall keep their distance and never rub on dogs.' There, take that."

"Ooo, how serious."

"You got that right, Kitty, and if you keep it up . . ."

His weird yellow eyes popped open. "Yes? Go on, Hankie. What might happen? I'm dying to hear this. I mean, it's not even eight o'clock yet and already you're in a world of trouble for," he gave me a wink, "tipping over the garbage barrels and scattering trash."

"I didn't do that, Pete. I was an innocent grandstander. Bystander. I was standing by innocently and did nothing wrong."

He moved up from my legs and began rubbing on my chest. "I know that, Hankie. I watched the whole thing from the iris patch. It's so sad that you got caught and blamed for what the coons did. I know it makes you angry."

"You bet it does. It was totally unjust and unfair."

"Uh-huh, and what makes it even worse is that . . ." He flicked his tail under my chin. ". . . what makes it really bad, Hankie, is that now I can do almost anything to you . . . and get by with it."

The growl in my throat increased in strength. "What do you mean by that, Kitty? Out with it. Let's get right to the point, if you have a point."

"Oh, I do, I do. See, you're already in so much

trouble, Hankie, that you don't dare get mad at me. What would Sally May think if I cried out in pain and started dragging my leg, hmmm?"

"She'd . . ." I drilled him with my gaze. "Pete, you're a despicable little creep."

"Yes I am, and I just love it."

"But I'm afraid it won't work."

"But it is working, Hankie. You're just aching to beat me up, aren't you? But you can't, can you?"

"Ha! That's what you think. I don't have to sit here and take trash off a cat. Do you know why, Pete? Because I can move."

"Try it."

"Sure, fine. I'll not only try it, I'll do it. Goodbye, I'm leaving."

And with that, I squared my shoulders and held my head at a proud angle and marched myself up to the machine shed, leaving Kitty Kitty in the shambles of his own rubble. By George, if I couldn't beat him up and chase him up a tree, at least I could walk away and claim a moral victory. Ha! Imagine him thinking that . . .

He followed me. The cat followed me!

At that very moment, Drover stuck his head out of the crack between the big sliding doors of the machine shed. He saw me and grinned. "Oh, hi, Hank. Sorry I had to leave the big fight, but

you know, this old leg went out on me and . . ."

"And so you left me to be blamed for the whole garbage mess, right? What a friend you turned out to be."

"Yeah, I was afraid that might happen, and I've been feeling pretty bad about it."

I shot a glance at Pete. He was still coming. "Uh, Drover, just how badly do you feel about it? I mean, running away from a combat situation and leaving a friend in his moment of greatest need?"

"Terrible, awful. The guilt has just been eating me up."

"No kidding. That bad, huh? Well, I know just the thing to solve this terrible problem of your guilt."

"You do? Oh good. How hard will it be?"

"Easy as pie. You see that cat coming in our direction?"

He turned his eyes to the east. "Oh yeah, that's Pete, good old Pete."

"Actually, Drover . . ." I studied the clouds for a moment. ". . . that's not Pete. It's a stray cat, an impostor, a cat that resembles Pete in many ways."

"Boy, you could have fooled me. He looks just like Pete."

"Uh-huh, I know, Drover, but he's not." I dropped my voice to a whisper. "He's a stray cat who's impersonating Pete."

"No fooling? Gosh, why would he do that?"

"We're not sure at this point, Drover. All I can tell you is that Pete has asked us, the elite members of the Security Division, his, uh, good friends, to beat up this impostor and run him off the ranch."

"I'll be derned."

"And we're looking for volunteers to, uh, do the job, so to speak."

"I'll be derned."

"And your name came to mind. It's a great honor. Congratulations."

"Yeah, but . . . I'm scared of cats."

"No problem, Drover. This cat is a patsy. You could whip him with one paw tied behind his back."

He grinned and stepped out of the machine shed. "Gosh, you really think so? I never whipped a cat before."

"This is your lucky day." I shot another glance at Mister Kitty Moocher. Heh, heh. He suspected nothing, had no idea that he was walking into the jaws of my trap. "Okay, here's the deal, Drover. You walk up to that cat and say, 'What's your name?' If he says his name is Pete, we'll know for sure that he's the impostor. I mean, what else would an impostor say?"

"Well, gosh, I never thought about that."

"It makes perfect sense. He wants us to think he's Pete, right? If he says he's Pete, he's lying. Jump right into the middle of him and beat the stuffings out of him. Don't hold anything back. And remember, this is for our friend Pete, good old Pete."

The little dunce jerked himself up to his full height. "You know what, Hank, I think I can do it, and I'm glad to do it for old Pete."

"That's the spirit. Go get 'im, Drover. There's liable to be a promotion in this."

"Oh goodie. Here I go."

I sat down to watch the show. Drover marched straight over to the cat and stuck his nose in Pete's face. I strained my ears to hear what he said. I could hardly wait.

"Hey, you," said Drover, "what's your name?"

Pete gave him a puzzled look, shot a glance at me, and turned his eyes back on Drover. And then he said—you won't believe this—with a big grin on his face, he said, "Genghis Khan."

HUH? The little dope. How could he have . . .

Drover beamed a smile and began wagging his stub tail. "Oh, hi, Pete. Gosh, there for a minute we thought you were someone else, but you're not and I don't have to beat you up. Come on, let's tell Hank. He'll be so proud."

And so the runt came rushing back to tell me the wonderful news. I ignored him. My eyes were on Pete. He was still grinning and purring, and he came straight to me and started rubbing on my legs.

"Hi, Hankie. It didn't work and I'm back."

Yes, he was back. It was my second defeat of the morning. You'll never guess what I did about that.

CHAPTER FIVE

I Embark on a New Career— as an Outlaw!

Drover must have noticed that a faraway look had come into my eyes, and that I wasn't celebrating the "success" of his mission.

"Hank? Hello? Gosh, I thought you'd be happy that I found old Pete and we're all together again." When I didn't respond, he moved into the path of my gaze. "Hello? Anybody home?"

Slowly, my thoughts returned to the present moment. I stared into Drover's face. "You don't understand, do you? No, of course not, so let me lay it out for you." I began pacing, mainly to keep the cat from rubbing the hair off my legs. "Drover, I've been disgraced and humiliated. It's no longer possible for me to carry on my duties as Head of Ranch Security. Therefore, as of this moment, I am resigning my position and leaving the ranch."

Drover's eyes almost bugged out of his head. He was struck speechless. Well, almost speechless. All he could say was, "Yeah but . . . yeah but . . . yeah but . . ."

A look of glee came over the cat's face. "Well, just darn the luck. I hope it wasn't something I did, Hankie."

I tried to ignore him. "Drover, I'm leaving the ranch in your hands."

"Yeah but . . . wait . . . help . . . oh my gosh, I don't even have any hands! All I've got is these paws and . . . I, I, I . . . I don't think I can handle this!" He lowered the front half of his body to the ground, raised his hiney in the air, and covered his eyes with his paws. "I'm not here. I've gone back to bed."

"Don't try to hide, Drover. It's time for you to step up to the plate."

"I've lost my appetite."

"Not a dinner plate, Drover, but the Home Plate of Life. You're in charge now. I'll leave you with one piece of advice. Stay away from the garbage barrels. Oh, and don't get too friendly with the cats."

"That's two pieces of advice, and I'm fixing to overload." I saw one of his eyes peeking out from between his paws. "Where will you go? What'll you do?"

"Oh," my gaze went to the far horizon, "you won't be proud to hear this, Drover, but I'm afraid that I'm going to become . . . an outlaw." I heard him gasp. "That's what happens to a dog when he tries to live by the rules and gets punished for it. Something happens, Drover. It kills something deep inside. It's a wound that won't heal, a pain that won't go away. Good-bye, son, and take good care of the ranch."

And with that, I turned and walked away—a broken dog, a dog who had tried his best but had failed. I had gone maybe thirty steps when I heard a voice behind me. I looked back and saw Pete, waving his paw and rubbing against Drover's leg.

Pete's parting words were, "Bye, Hankie. Cats rule."

Many thoughts marched across the parade ground of my mind. The main thought was that I should have hamburgerized the cat when I had the chance. Heck, I was leaving anyway. I should have left with one last burst of pleasure. But I put this thought and all the others out of my mind. Pete wasn't my problem any more.

I was a free dog! No more worries or cares, no more eighteen-hour days, no more crushing responsibility. I pointed myself toward the west, turned my back on the ranch I had loved and protected, and went marching into a new life . . . as an outlaw.

Pretty exciting, huh? I thought so. I couldn't wait to throw myself into the task of living off the land. I would eat fresh rabbit twice a day, and wild fruits and berries and nuts, gathered from Nature's own supermarket. No more tasteless dog food kernels out of a sack for me. Shucks, this was going to be a blast, and I wondered why I hadn't done it sooner.

Pete didn't know it, but he had done me a huge favor by pushing me over the brink of the edge.

I made my way down to the creek and followed it in a westerly direction. Soon, all the familiar landmarks disappeared and I found myself in new country, wild country that touched the savage depths of my savage heart. I was already hungry, so I put my nose to the groundstone and went right to work, applying my vast skills as a tracker, hunter, stalker, and liver-off-the-lander.

It didn't take me long to pick up the scent of a rabbit and within minutes I had followed this tender, juicy little bunny to a hole in the ground.

Yes sir, I had him cornered. All that remained was for me to put the old claws to work and dig the little feller out.

Two hours later I, uh, had excavated a huge pile of dirt and . . . rabbits aren't as easy to dig out of holes as you might have suspected, see, and this one appeared to be pretty safe in . . . who'd have thought that a shrimpy little rabbit could . . .

Phooey. I'd never cared much for the taste of rabbit anyway. Nuts and berries, that's what I needed. Nuts and berries and certain roots that were known only to dogs who had finished the course in Wilderness Survival.

I abandoned the rabbit chase and began shopping for tidbits and morsels that were . . . well, in short supply, you might say. I mean, this was the Texas Panhandle, after all, not the Garden of Eating, and yes, it did take me a while to locate a plump, juicy root that promised to silence the growling in my stomach.

But at last I found one, a plump, juicy white root of the soapweed plant. I crunched into it. Great texture, nice crunchy texture, and by George, once I had adjusted to the first taste, I began to . . .

Spit it out. Gag! It tasted like SOAP! No wonder they called it soapweed. How foolish of me . . . but there were other plants out here, hundreds of them, and other animals had figured out how to survive. Surely I could too. So I threw myself into the task, hunting and foraging, digging and tasting, and by the end of the day . . .

Okay, let's face the truth. I was starving and I had found a new respect for any animal that could survive in the wild. Was I missing something? Everything tasted like wood or dirt. Or soap. If this was a preview of life on the Outlaw Trail, fellers, I might have to rethink my plans for the future.

Well, my spirits had just about hit the bottom and I was walking along, looking at all the trees and bushes that weren't fit to eat, when all at once I saw a bush move up ahead. Ah ha, maybe, just maybe, I had found myself a bunny rabbit who wasn't twenty feet down in the earth—a rabbit, in other words, who could be chased and caught in the normal manner.

Have we discussed my position on rabbits? I love 'em. Sometimes they're hard to catch, but they're delicious, and boy, was I ready for a nice rabbit dinner. I threw all circuits over into Stealthy Crouch Mode and began the Stalking Procedure.

This required a great deal of patience. I'll be the first to admit that patience had never been one of my, uh, more obvious qualities. I mean, when your mind operates at a high rate of speed, when it's filled with plans and grand thoughts, it's hard to adjust to the slow rhythms of a brainless bunny rabbit.

But my weeks of surviving in the wilderness had . . . okay, *hours,* but they had been the longest hours of my life . . . my long hours of surviving in the wilderness had forced patience upon me, and I began stalking the rabbit with all the patience of a wild aminal. Animal. Beast.

I put my nose to the ground and went to work. Yes, there was a scent, the very clear scent of a rabbit, and the farther I went, the heavier and wilder the scent became. This must be a pretty wild rabbit, because he sure had left a . . .

HUH?

I went to Full Air Brakes and shut everything down. I froze in my tracks and cut my eyes from side to side. I could feel a strip of hair rising along my backbone, all the way out to the end of my tail.

You know that scent we were following? That scent you thought belonged to a "wild rabbit," to use your exact words? Get ready for a shock. That scent had nothing to do with rabbits, but it had a lot to do with COYOTES. See, at certain times and under certain circumstances, the scent of a rabbit is hard to distinguish from . . .

Let's just say that we'd gotten some faulty readings on our instruments, and they had put us on the trail of some of the worst villains in the country. I was out there *playing outlaw,* but the guys whose scent I was following didn't just play. They *were* outlaws, the real McCall. And suddenly my appetite for the Outlaw Trail began to shrink, and if I could just back myself out of there without making a sound . . .

Oops. Who had put that bush right in my path? Surely it hadn't been there before, but it was now and I brushed against it and one of the branches snapped. I flattened myself out on the ground and lay perfectly . . .

Eyes? Yipes, I suddenly realized that I was being stared at by two yellow, wolfish eyes. Who on the ranch had such "yellow, wolfish eyes"? Gulp. Rip and Snort, the notorious coyote brothers.

But wait a second. Rip and Snort had two eyes apiece, and two eyes plus two eyes equals four eyes, right? Yet I was seeing just two eyes, so . . . hmmm. Somehow the math . . .

Ah ha, but then I saw the tail, a long fluffy coyote tail, and that made it all work out. Don't you get it? I was seeing Rip's eyes and Snort's tail, or Snort's eyes and Rip's tail, so that made the math come out right.

Two coyotes. Rip and Snort. Gulp.

I flattened myself even flatter on the ground. Maybe they would think I was a . . . I don't know what, maybe a snake. Yes, maybe they would think I was a snake in the grass.

I had blundered right into Rip and Snort's territory. And if a guy could choose where he was blundering, he would never choose to blunder into their company. I mean, they were thugs. I knew 'em pretty well, and one of the things I knew about them was that, if given the opportunity, they just might eat a ranch dog for supper.

Pretty scary, huh? You bet it was. What a lousy deal, what a sorry turn of events. I had been minding my own business, stalking my next meal, but it appeared that I might become *their* next meal.

Oh brother. Could I get out of this?

It looked pretty hopeless. I mean, there wasn't a chance that I could hotfoot it back to the ranch. Nobody outruns Rip and Snort. You might as well try to outrun your own shadow. They had eyes that saw everything. Their ears heard every tiny sound. And they had noses that could track an ant in total darkness.

Gulk.

It appeared that my best hope, my only hope, was to try a different approach. Hencely, instead of trying to run or hide, I pushed myself up to a standing position and turned to the eyes that had been watching me.

"Well, by George, it's Rip and Snort! Where have you been, fellas? I've been looking for you all afternoon."

Well, prepare yourself for another shock. It wasn't Rip and Snort.

Do you suppose it might be the Garbage Monster from Outer Space? You'll just have to keep reading and find out.

CHAPTER SIX

Holy Smokes, a Lovely Coyote Princess!

You'll never believe who it was. Even I was surprised. Are you ready? Here goes.

It was Missy Coyote. Do you remember her? The lovely coyote princess, the daughter of Chief Many-Rabbit-Gut-Eat-in-Full-Moon, and the sister of Scraunch the Terrible. I hadn't seen her in a long time, and fellers, when I did, I just melted.

I mean, part of the melting deal came from relief that she wasn't Rip and Snort, but most of it came from the fact that she was . . . WOW! She was so gorgeous and beautiful, I couldn't believe my eyes or my good fortune.

See, she had this necklace of soft fluffy hair

around her neck, a long bushy tail, an awesome nose, and a pair of eyes that were . . . hmm, hard to describe. I mean, they were yellowish eyes, not one of my favorite colors in women's eyes, and yes, they had a certain wolfish quality about them, but somehow they were softly wolfish and softly yellow.

Sorry, that's the best I can do. You'll just have to take my word for it. Those were some amazing eyes.

I must have gawked at her for a whole minute. I hated to gawk and stare, but what's a guy to do when he's out tramping in the wilderness and comes face-to-face with a coyote princess? You gawk and stare, that's what you do.

After a while she cocked her head to the side and smiled. "That you, Hunk?"

"I think it's me. It was me the last time I checked, but that was before I was blinded by the sunlight of your moonbeam."

She gave a little laugh. "That not make sense, sunlight of moonbeam."

"Right, but it's the best I can do right now. I think I just fell down the stairwell of love, Missy, and I'm still rolling."

"Hunk talk funny."

"Yeah, but it's a miracle that I can talk at all. I mean, have you ever looked at yourself in a pool of water? Do you have any idea how gorgeous you are?"

"What means 'gorgeous'?"

"It means beautiful, lovely, awesome, terrific, splendiferous. The kind of face that causes hearts to stop beating, ice to melt, birds to faint and fall out of trees. The kind of face that causes a dog like me to forget who he is and where he came from, how to walk and talk."

"Oh, Hunk make big foolish with talk of gorgeous. Missy's face just a face, a place for hanging nose and mouth and ears."

"Ha! That's what you think."

Her expression darkened. "But what Hunk doing out here in wild place? Not safe for ranch dog, away from people-friends and boom-boom."

"Hey, Missy, I've left all that stuff behind. I quit my lousy job and ran away to become . . . well, an outlaw or something. What do you think of that?"

She was quiet for a moment. "Missy think Hunk not really care for life of outlaw, belong with people-friends and house. Outlaw life pretty hard for dog, Missy think."

"You really think so? What's so hard about this? I mean, here I am enjoying a nice fall afternoon, looking at the trees, and talking with the most beautiful coyote princess in the world. Nobody's mad at me or blaming me for crimes I didn't commit. I'm not listening to Drover's brainless conversations or taking trash off the cat. Where's the problem?"

At that moment, my stomach cranked out a loud growl. Missy heard it, cocked her head to the side, and smiled. "Hunk hungry for food?"

"Okay, food might be a small problem on the outlaw trail, I'll admit it, but heck, you coyotes live out here all the time and seem to get along fine. Maybe," I wiggled my left eyebrow at her, "maybe you could teach me how to live off the land, huh?

I've got all the time in the world and . . . heh, heh . . . I'd just love to be the teacher's pet."

"Hunk might not like what coyote eat."

"Hey, Missy, food's only food, right? Anything a coyote can eat, a dog can eat too. No problem."

"But Missy not good teacher on hunt for food. Rip and Snort much better."

"Yeah, but Rip and Snort aren't here—which, by the way, doesn't exactly break my heart."

"Rip and Snort not far away."

"Oh? Hmm. Then maybe you and I could sort of fade into the wilderness and ditch them, so to speak. I don't want to bad-mouth your friends or kinfolks, Missy, but those guys . . . how can I say this? One day we seem to be pals, and the next time they look at me with these hungry eyes, almost as though they'd like to . . . well, eat me."

Missy chirped a little laugh. "Rip and Snort just good old boy coyotes."

We shared a laugh together. "Right. They're good old boys, Missy, but my feelings about them would change if they were to eat me."

"Not eat Hunk. Missy have talk with brothers, tell brothers be nice to Hunk while Hunk learn outlaw way."

"Yes, either that or you and I could slip away and . . ."

"Shhh!" Her head came up and she swiveled one of her lovely pointed ears toward the west. She listened and sniffed the wind. "Rip and Snort coming now."

"Bummer." She shot a glance at me. "I mean, good. How swell. Now I can learn survival techniques from two of the . . ." She wasn't listening so I finished the thought under my breath. ". . . two of the meanest cannibals in Texas. Bummer."

Missy's ears were quite a bit keener than mine, and she had picked up the approach of the brothers long before I heard anything. But soon I heard them coming. They sounded like . . . elephants. Buffalo. A herd whole of cattle, whole herd of cattle, snapping brush and tearing limbs from trees. And singing.

Yes, they were singing. I think that's what they were doing. It was hard to tell, they were such dreadful singers. But here they came, crashing through the brush and bellering their latest piece of coyote trash. Let's see if I can remember how it went.

Oh Boy

Oh boy, oh boy, our hearts are full of joy.
We stomp around and play all night,

Disturb the peace till day's first light
And if we're lucky we'll pick a fight ...
Oh boy, oh boy, oh boy.

Well, me and Rip are cannibal lads, we
    always have a blast.
When it comes to fights and wrecking things,
    we're surely unsurpassed.
Some guys might think we're stupid, just
    because we act that way.
It ain't an act, we really are, and here is
    what we say:

Oh boy, oh boy, our hearts are full of joy.
We stomp around and play all night,
Disturb the peace till day's first light
And if we're lucky we'll pick a fight ...
Oh boy, oh boy, oh boy.

Perhaps you think we ain't too proud of
    being igno-rent.
Well, we've got news for you, and boy, you'd
    better take the hint.
We're prouder and proudest of what we are,
    we work at it every day.
We burp and scratch and pick our nose, and
    here is what we say:

Oh boy, oh boy, our hearts are full of joy.
We stomp around and play all night,
Disturb the peace till day's first light
And if we're lucky we'll pick a fight . . .
Oh boy, oh boy, oh boy.

The thing that we are proudest of is our tal-
　　ent for fighting skunks.
They've sprayed us several hundred times,
　　and boy, we've really stunks.
But here's the deal, we love the smell
　　because it actually may
Attract the coyote gals in droves, and here is
　　what we say:

Oh boy, oh boy, our hearts are full of joy.
We stomp around and play all night,
Disturb the peace till day's first light,
And if we're lucky we'll pick a fight . . .
Oh boy, oh boy, oh boy.

Pretty bad, huh? I tried to warn you.

They came tromping into camp and marched in
a circle around me and Missy, singing at the top of
their lungs. I was tempted to cover my ears to keep
them from being damaged by the noise, but of
course I didn't do that. I mean, when you're with

cannibals, you don't wish to seem disrespectful of their . . . uh . . . cultural heritage, so to speak.

There were probably a couple of coyote mothers in the world who could have listened to such trash . . . uh, singing . . . expressions of cultural so forth . . . and might have actually beamed with pride. Motherhood is blind, they say, and might also be deaf, and it's just possible that the mothers of Rip and Snort might have appreciated their singing.

Not me. I turned to Missy and was about to whisper something about the noise . . . but was shocked to see her hanging on every note and word. Her eyes were sparkling and she was mouthing the words and her paws were clasped in front of her, as though she thought this was something wonderful.

Hmmm. It appeared that Missy and I had a few . . . uh . . . differences.

Well, the guys finished the song and began whooping and hollering. Missy rushed out and gave each of them a hug. I was sure it meant nothing, almost nothing at all, just a little token gesture to make them feel better about . . . okay, maybe she actually liked their song and, yes, this did give further proof that there might be a few differences between coyotes and . . . well, dogs, you might say.

But they were small differences, tiny differences, nothing that couldn't be solved and overcome.

Whilst they celebrated their noisy song, I more or less sat off to myself. I checked the claws on my right paw, studied the clouds, and went after a flea that was crawling around on my hind leg. Then, suddenly, I realized that the shouting and laughing had died out and a deep silence had moved in.

I stopped biting at the flea and turned my gaze toward the brothers. They seemed to be ... well, staring at me. I thought nothing of it and went back to chasing the flea.

But then I heard Snort's booming voice, and it got my full undivided attention. In his booming voice, Snort said—and this is a direct quote—he said:

"Uh! Coyote girl do good, catch ranch dog out in weirderness. Rip and Snort play and sing all day, ready now for big yummy coyote feast, oh boy!"

HUH?

Coyote feast? Surely they weren't thinking of ...

Holy smokes, this wasn't what I'd had in mind, not at all.

CHAPTER SEVEN

I Enroll in
Rip and Snort's
Wilderness School

J ust for a second there, I thought I had been betrayed by the lovely Missy Coyote.

On the one hand, it was hard to believe she might have resisted my many charms, and we're talking about, oh, massive shoulders, a pretty nice coat of hair, dashing good looks, great talent, a wonderful charming personality, dashing good looks, nice ears, a heck of a fine nose, and dashing good looks.

On the other hand . . . she was a coyote and I was a dog, and when push came to shovel, she just might choose her own kind over me. And that would not be good.

That would be very bad, and I found myself studying the paths and trails that led back to the ranch, just in case this deal got out of hand.

But then I noticed that Missy was talking to the brothers. They were listening but didn't appear to be real happy about it. I heard several loud grunts and growls, and then Snort said, "Rip and Snort not want dummy ranch dog for teaching. Want dummy ranch dog for supper!"

The conference went on for several more minutes. I tried not to show a great amount of concern, even though I was getting worried. I mean, Missy was the chief's daughter and had some influence, but when you're dealing with cannibals, you never know how things might turn out.

At last the conference broke up. Snort came pounding over to where I was sitting. His face was . . . sour, shall we say. He didn't look happy at all. He marched up to me and poked me in the chest with his paw.

"Coyote girl say she friend of Hunk."

"Oh? Well, thanks. Yes, we've been . . ."

"Rip and Snort not give a hoot for dummy ranch dog and not want teach dummy ranch dog coyote ways."

"Yes, well, I can understand . . ."

"Ranch dog shut trap and listen."

"Yes sir."

He kept poking me in the chest. "Rip and Snort take dummy ranch dog for big night of hunt and tear-up, but only for coyote girl."

"Well, that's very kind of you, Snort."

He poked me again. "Ha! Not kind. Coyote not give a hoot for kind."

"Do you suppose we could discuss this without you, uh, poking a hole in my rib cage?"

"Snort not give a hoot for ripped cage."

"Rib cage."

"Shut trap."

"Yes sir."

"Rip and Snort take dog along, but Hunk got to pass test, ha ha."

I stared into his wicked yellow eyes. "Test? What sort of test did you, uh, have in mind?"

He puffed himself up. "Hunk have to sing Coyote Sacred Hymnal and National Anthemum—all by self."

"Oh, you mean 'Me Just a Worthless Coyote'? Let's see . . . yes, I think I can remember the words. But of course I'll do my own arrangement and it might not sound as bad . . . that is, it might not sound as good as what you guys do."

"Ha. Too bad. Hunk sing."

The brothers plopped themselves down on the

ground and stared at me with eyes that ex-
pressed . . . well, a small amount of anger but
mostly boredom. Yes, large amounts of boredom,
almost as though they were doing this strictly as
a favor to Missy—which they were.

Well, this wouldn't be so bad. I mean, I'd heard
Rip and Snort do the song many times, and I'd even
sung it with them a few times. As a test of my skills
and abilities, this promised to be no big deal. I tuned
my tonsils and banged out a great new arrangement of their shabby little National Anthem.

Coyote Sacred Hymn and National Anthem

Me just a worthless coyote, me howling at
    the moon.
Me like to sing and holler, me crazy as a loon.
Me not want job or duties, no church or
    Sunday school,
Me just a worthless coyote, but me ain't
    nobody's fool.

I did in it waltz time, see, gave it a snappy little
rhythm, added some harmony parts, and generally
spiffed it up. It turned out to be a huge improve-
ment over the dreary thing they usually sang.

When I was finished, I turned to the audience

and bowed. Missy gave a squeal of delight and clapped her paws. The brothers continued staring at me, I mean, their expressions hadn't changed one bit.

"Thanks, Missy. Well, what do you think, guys? Not bad, huh?"

Snort swiped his paw through the air. "Trash."

"Oh, well . . . sorry. I thought you might appreciate the new arrangement. I'm sure you'll agree that—"

"Snort not agree for nothing. Snort madder and maddest for being nice to dummy ranch dog. And Snort hungry too, wanting to eat and burp and fight and tear up whole world." The brothers stood up and shook the grass off their coats. "Hunk follow."

"Well, sure, but I want you to know that—"

"And Hunk shut stupid mouth too. Talk too much." He headed west, down a cow path, and I could hear him grumbling to himself. "Not want to listening dummy ranch dog talk all night. Coyote not give hoot for . . . mumble, grumble, mutter."

I fell in behind Snort, and noticed that Missy wasn't following. In fact, she was waving her paw good-bye. "Hey, you're not going with us?"

"No. Coyote boys go for big hunt and fun. Missy wait."

I stopped. "Uh, listen, is there a chance I could stay with you? I mean, Rip and Snort are charming guys and all, but I wouldn't mind . . ."

She shook her head. "Hunk go with brothers, learn outlaw ways with outlaws."

"Yes, of course. And you're pretty sure they won't try to eat me, right?" She nodded. "Great. Well, this is what I wanted . . . I guess. See you around, Missy."

Darkness was falling and I plunged into the growing shadows and caught up with my . . . whatever they were. My teachers in outlawry and survival methods.

I wondered what Drover was doing. And Pete. And Little Alfred. Not that I missed them, understand. It was just that . . . okay, maybe I missed them, but not much. Surely the adventure and excitement of becoming an outlaw dog would . . .

I followed Rip and Snort into the uncharted wilderness. This was going to be fun, great fun. I just knew it would be.

We followed the trail for, oh, half a mile, I'd say, and then we left the trail and began marching through some tall grass near the creek. This was the fall of the year, don't you know, and the country had raised a big crop of sandburs that summer. All at once I found myself limping and hopping. Those sandburs were tearing me up.

"Say, fellas, could we stop for a second and let me pull some of these stickers out of my paws?"

I sat down and began gnawing at the stickers in my left front paw. I got those out and had moved to the rear when Snort came up behind me.

"Hunk not stop in middle of march."

"Yes, well, I seem to have . . . didn't you guys notice all these sandburs?"

"Ha! Coyote berry tough guys, not give a hoot for little sticker-hurt in foots." He kicked me in the tail section. "Hunk get tough, too."

I leaped to my . . . youch . . . feet. "Sure, you bet. No problem."

We resumed the march. My feet were killing me! I tried to walk on crumpled toes, on the sides of my feet, on my elbows, but those stickers were eating me alive. But I didn't dare complain or say a word.

You think those guys weren't tough? They were tough.

We marched for another five minutes or so, and then Snort called a halt. He came back to the rear of the column where I was, shall we say, unstick-ering my paws again. He glared down at me.

"Uh. Hunk got soft foots."

"No, actually I think they're getting tougher

by the, uh, minute. No kidding. Tougher and tougher. I can almost feel the change."

"Hunk got soft foots, never become outlaw dog with soft foots."

"Don't worry about it, Snort. My feet will be fine."

"Not feet. Foots."

"Okay, foots. My foots will be fine."

"Not fine. Foots soft."

"Okay, my foots are soft, but they'll be fine."

"Ha. Better be." He pointed a paw to a spot of soft ground in front of us. "Now Hunk use soft foots for dig up supper."

My spirits rose on hearing "supper." "Hey, great. This is the part I've been looking forward to all day. And you said . . . dig?"

He scowled and raised his voice. "DIG. Use foots for shovel, make hole in ground."

"Right. I understand the meaning of 'dig' but I was a little surprised . . ."

He clubbed me over the head with his paw. "Hunk talk too much. Use foots for dig and never mind surprising. Rip and Snort watch, ho ho."

"Okay, fine, I can handle digging."

And so I began digging. It wasn't bad. The ground was soft and moist and before long I had a nice little hole. The only problem was that I had

no idea what I was digging for. Roots? That seemed a likely possibility, only there weren't any roots in this particular area. I thought of asking about this but decided against it.

While I was doing all the work, the brothers sat nearby, grinning and belching. They seemed pretty proud of their belching skills, and each tried to outdo the other. I would have been more impressed if they had lent a hand with the digging, but that didn't seem to be in their plans. They didn't mind letting me do all the work.

I must have dug for fifteen solid minutes and it had just about worn me out. When I stopped to catch my breath, they noticed. Snort lumbered over and studied the pile of fresh dirt beside the hole.

"Ah ha! Hunk find good grub, oh boy. Now Hunk get to eat."

"Hey, great, thanks. Yes, I'm starved." I climbed out of the hole, shook some dirt out of my hair, and stared down at the dirt pile. Hmm. I couldn't see anything but . . . I looked closer. My head came up and I gave Snort a puzzled look.

"Grub worms?"

CHAPTER EIGHT

I Am Forced
to Eat Grub Worms

Snort's face wadded itself up into a scowl. "Hunk not like coyote grub?

"Oh no, it's not that, not at all. It's just . . . you guys eat *grub worms*? I mean, I thought coyotes ate fresh rabbit . . . ground squirrels . . . prairie dogs . . . you know, good nourishing meat dishes that are, uh, nourishing and fresh and so forth."

"Grubber worms plenty fresh, still wiggle when coyote crunch up."

"No kidding? They're, uh, still wiggling when you chew them up?"

"Plenty fresh. Also crunch and pop in mouth, oh boy." Perhaps he saw my eyes cross. "Hunk not like crunch and pop?"

"I didn't say that, Snort. It's just that . . . well,

I . . . I've never eaten grub worms before, is the point. They're not part of a dog's . . . cultural experience, shall we say, and I just have no idea . . . ha ha . . . how a guy might go about . . . eating them, don't you see."

"Uh. Rip show Hunk how to eat yummy grubber worm."

Rip flashed a big grin and stepped up to the dirt pile. He picked around in the dirt with his paw until he found a nice fat worm. Then he pitched it up into the air, caught it in his jaws, and slammed them shut. The first sound we heard was the snap of his jaws. This was followed an instant later by a pop—which sent a little tremor through my innards.

Rip chewed it up, grinned, and said, "Uh!"

Snort turned back to me. "Brother say grubber worm yummy and yummiest. Now Hunk give try for eating yummy grub."

"You know, Snort, I ate right before I left the ranch, and gee whiz, I don't think I could hold another bite. No kidding."

He glared at me with his empty yellow eyes. "Gee whiz better eat coyote food or coyote brothers get madder and maddest."

"Right, that's just what I was thinking. We sure don't want to insult anyone's . . . uh . . . cultural heritage, do we?"

I picked through the dirt and found the smallest, skinniest worm in the bunch. Snort watched my every move and shook his head. "Too skinny for guest. Hunk pick bigger and fattest of all. Take this one."

He pointed his paw to the biggest, fattest, ugliest, nastiest yucko-worm of them all. I squeezed up a weak smile, swallowed hard, and said, "Well, here goes. Over the teeth, over the gums, look out stomach, here it comes."

I pitched it up, caught it, and crunched it. It popped. It oozed. I could feel it spreading across my tongue and mouth, like a spill of toxic garbage juice. I had no intention of swallowing that slime. I would hold it in my mouth, heh heh, until they weren't looking, then I would . . .

The boys were smiling. "Pretty yummy, huh?"

"Oh ess. Icks eeyishus. I yuv it."

"Ha! Then swallow."

He whopped me on the back and . . . gulk . . . I felt the toxic green slime sliding down my food pipe and invading the quiet happiness of my stomach. My upper lip curled. My eyes crossed.

My pals saw it all. I got the impression that they even enjoyed it. "Pretty yummy, huh? Eat more."

I could hardly speak. My eyes were watering. My tongue, mouth, and taste buds had just been

poisoned. I gasped for breath. "Oh, you guys go ahead."

"*Hunk eat more.*"

"Right. You bet."

And so, with the wolf-eyed brotherhood hovering over me and watching my every move and gesture, I did my duty. The first five were the worst. The second five were bad enough but some better. By that time, all the circuits in my tongue and mouth had been fried beyond recognition, and my stomach had already gone into convulsions and shock.

The Brotherhood observed it all and seemed pleased. Snort whopped me on the back again. "Uh! Hunk like coyote food, huh?"

I smiled and gazed at them through bleary eyes. "Oh yeah, you bet. Those worms are . . . Snort, has your face always been green? Uh-oh. 'Scuse me, boys, I've got to . . ."

I dashed into the bushes and put the worms back where they belonged—on the ground. When I staggered back to the brothers, they were shaking their heads.

"Hunk cheat, not make good coyote. Better try again."

"No, fellas, please, no more. It's not that I don't like your . . . okay, let's admit the truth. Worms make me sick. There it is. I thought I was dog enough to eat anything you ate, but I was wrong."

They stared at me. "Hunk flunk."

"Ha. That rhymes, doesn't it? You know, guys, words are very . . ."

"Not change subject. Hunk flunk test."

"No, wait, I think I can . . . okay, I flunked the test. Where do we go from here?"

They went into a whispering conference. Then, "Maybe we try Hunk in one more test—and better not flunk."

Whew! I almost fainted with relief. There for a

second, I'd thought my cook was goosed. "Hey, great, no problem. I'll do better on this one, you'll see."

"Uh. Better do better."

"What will we be doing this time? I mean, I was hoping it wouldn't involve . . . well, worms, you might say."

"Hunk find out soon enough." They looked at each other and laughed. Then Snort gave the order for us to move out.

I fell in line behind them, and away we marched through the bushes and darkness. It was the same formation we had followed before—Snort out front, then Rip, then me—and from outward appearances, nothing had changed.

But something HAD changed. It suddenly occurred to me that these guys were never going to give me a test that I could pass. They were never going to accept me as one of their own, because . . . well, because I wasn't.

What a blockhead I'd been, leaving the ranch, leaving my job, my friends, my gunnysack bed . . . and yes, even my bowl of tasteless dog food. All at once leaving the ranch seemed about the dumbest move I'd ever made. Sure, I'd been blamed for the garbage barrel fiasco, but so what? With Sally May and Loper and Slim, at least a guy had a chance to repair the damage and try again on a better day. But with Rip and Snort . . .

Right then, at that very moment, I knew what I had to do. I had to get out of there. I had to escape, run back to my ranch and hope that I could take up where I'd left off. It wouldn't be easy, but I had a plan.

See, I was the last in line, right? I'd been in the caboose position all night and the brothers hadn't paid any attention to me. All I had to do was slow my pace just a bit, fall behind, and then make a run for it. I would head straight to the creek and swim downstream for a hundred yards or so. That would cover my scent.

Pretty smart, huh? You bet it was. See, Rip and Snort were the champs when it came to following a scent on dry land, but even they couldn't pick up a trail through water. All I needed was two minutes' head start, and I just might be able to pull it off.

I slowed my pace, just a tiny bit at first, then a little more and a little more. So far, so good. I stopped and listened. I could hear them marching on to the west. Great. It was working. Now, all I had to do was turn and . . .

HUH? I ran smack-dab into a big hairy cannibal.

It was Snort. He gave me a toothy grin. "Hunk get lost in dark?"

"I . . . I . . . I . . . yes, yes, and I was just about to,

uh, call for help. Boy, am I glad you showed up."

"Hunk change mind about outlaw trail?"

"Me? Change my . . . ha ha . . . surely you're joking, Snort. Me, change my mind about . . . hey, who'd want to go back to the dull routine of ranch life? Not me, no sir. Okay, maybe eating grub worms isn't my idea of . . . why are you staring at me?"

He was staring at me. "Hunk not leave, still got big test."

"Right, and I wouldn't miss it for the world, Snort. Honest. No kidding. I mean, I just love a challenge."

"Hunk march between Rip and Snort, not get lost."

"Great idea. I was about to . . . there's no need to push and shove, Snort, really. See? I'm marching. Here we go, off on a new adventure."

Good grief, had he read my mind? My plans for escaping had just gone down in flames. Gulp. Now what was I going to do? It appeared that I had become a captive.

And so it was with a heavy heart that I fell into line between the cannibal brothers. Snort followed me like a shadow and never took his eyes off me. When he thought my pace was too slow, he bit me on the tail. As you might guess, that gave me a powerful desire to keep moving.

We marched westward for another half hour or so, and then we came to a stop. I glanced around, studied landmarks, and tried to figure out where we were. My best guess was that we had tramped through the horse pasture and were now inside Wolf Creek Park. Yes, of course we were because up ahead, I could see several camp sites with tents and travel trailers.

People came here to camp and fish in the lake, don't you see. That's why *people* came to the park, but why would a couple of rowdy coyotes come here? I mean, coyotes tried to stay away from people, right? It didn't make much sense to me. There was something fishy about this.

I waited for the brothers to make the next move. They went into a huddle. They whispered and muttered for several minutes, then Snort came over to me.

"Hunk ready for next big test?"

"You bet, sure, no problem. But Snort, allow me to point out that we're standing in the middle of a public park. People camp here, see, a lot of people, and in a few hours they'll be waking up. Maybe you didn't realize that."

He gave me a blank stare. "Many people make many garbage."

"Yes, that's true."

"Many garbage have plenty food."

"Oh sure, but . . . wait a minute, whoa, hold it, halt. Surely you're not thinking of . . ."

For Pete's sake, my life had come full circle. They wanted to raid the garbage barrels!

CHAPTER NINE

Garbage Barrels Again

They were standing over me now, both of them grinning. Snort spoke. "Now Hunk show coyote brothers how to work big garbage deal, ho ho."

"Wait a minute, Snort. You mean this is the next test?" They nodded. "Raiding garbage barrels in a public park?" They nodded. "Are you guys crazy?" They nodded.

I got up and started pacing. "Fellas, listen to your old buddy Hank. You're the experts on wilderness survival—fighting badgers, beating up skunks, eating grub worms, and so forth—but you don't know much about people, so let me give you a lesson.

"Number one, people take a very dim view of animals who tip over garbage barrels in public places. Number two, they're likely to shoot animals who do it. Number three, coons get by with it because they are cute little fellers. Number four, you and I are not cute. And Number five, we could get ourselves shot." I stopped pacing and paused a moment for dramatic effect. "That's as plain as I can make it, guys. I'm sure you'll agree that it's much too dangerous."

They shook their heads. "Coyote not scared, 'cause coyote got plan."

"*You* have a plan?"

"Yeah. Got good plan. Work pretty good too."

"Snort, somehow..." I heaved a sigh. "I've known you guys for ... how many years? And you've never planned anything. Okay, let's hear the plan."

"Ha! Coyote hide in weeds and let Hunk tip over barrels, then coyote move in for big yummy feast. Pretty good plan, huh?"

My eyes darted from one face to the other. Were they joking? No. Coyotes had no sense of humor and they never joked. They were serious about this.

"Wait a minute. You think I'm going to ... ha ha, I don't think so, guys. No way. Listen, I've already been to school on this garbage barrel stuff and ..."

"Hunk take big test. If Hunk do good, maybe become outlaw brother."

"Yeah, right, or maybe I'll stop a couple of loads of buckshot."

They shrugged. "Life pretty tough, all right."

I began pacing again. "One question, guys. Do I have a choice here?" They shook their heads. "That's what I thought." I had reached the east end of my pacing range. "In that case, I think I'll . . ."

I made a run for it. I didn't think it would work. It didn't. Those guys were faster than greased lightning bugs. Before I knew it, they were stacked on top of me, and I found myself not only getting smashed, but also looking into Snort's face.

"What Hunk say now?"

"I say that your plan stinks. Furthermore, you're smashing me."

"Ha. Snort not give a hoot for smush Hunk dog. Coyote get mad and smush whole world."

"Okay, then let me point out that Missy wouldn't approve of this."

"Ha. Missy not here, only Rip and Snort."

"Okay. Well, what the heck, let's, uh, crack open a few garbage barrels and see what we can find. I haven't been shot at in a couple of months. It might be fun."

They unpiled and let me up. I noticed that they were looking . . . unfriendly. Hostile. Their ears were pinned down, their fangs were showing, and the hair on their backs was standing up. Those were all bad signs.

Snort stuck his nose in my face. "Hunk better not try run off again."

"Me, run off? No problem. Hey, I wouldn't miss this for the world." Snort glared at me and pointed a paw toward three garbage barrels nearby. "So, uh, just tip 'em over, is that right?" He nodded. "All three?" He nodded. "And what if someone comes out of that camper trailer and starts shooting? Do we have a plan for that?" He shook his head. "Listen, weren't we supposed to go back and find Missy?" He shook his head. "Well," I took a deep gulp of air, "here we go."

While the brothers hid behind some bushes, I marched over to the three barrels, hopped up on my back legs, hooked my paws over the rims, and tipped them over. Each barrel hit the ground with a loud clunk that broke the silence of the night. I cringed on each clunk, and cast worried glances toward the trailer nearby.

If somebody in there woke up and came outside and got a look at me and notified the park ranger . . . I didn't even want to think about it.

Can you imagine? Loper would get an angry call first thing in the morning. "Hey, your dog's over here in the park, tipping over trash barrels!"

It would look very bad, especially since I had already been blamed for one mess that day.

How did I get myself into these deals? Me, an innocent dog who'd never had the slightest interest in exploring garbage barrels. Okay, maybe I'd toppled a few on my own, but that had been long ago. I'd learned my lessons and had kept a clean record, but now . . .

It was all Pete's fault. He would pay for this . . . if I happened to survive.

I shot another glance at the trailer. No lights came on. Maybe I would get lucky this time, tend to the dirty business, escape from Rip and Snort, return home to the ranch, and get on with my life. And give Pete the pounding he deserved.

The brothers waited until they were sure the coast was clear. Then they came creeping out of the shadows. As Snort walked past me, he tossed me a grin and said, "Uh. Hunk pretty good garbage dog."

"Thanks. If I'm so good, maybe you could pitch me a bone or a scrap. I'm starved."

"Ha! Hunk pretty funny too. Rip and Snort take care of bone and scrap stuff. Hunk eat grubber worm, ha ha."

They both got big chuckles out of that "grubber worm" business. I didn't think it was so funny myself. My mouth still tasted awful.

The brothers licked their chops and dived into one of the barrels. I watched and listened as they scratched and clawed their way through the papers and cans, searching for morsels of food. As I sat there, it suddenly occurred to me that . . . hmm, they were both inside the barrel, right? And I was sitting outside the barrel, all alone, right? Maybe I could just . . .

Snort's head popped out of the barrel. He gave me a vicious look. "Hunk not move. Hunk not even think about move."

"Me? Move? No sir, Snort, I'm right here, standing guard for, uh, you guys. That's my job, right? Don't worry about a thing. If I see anything suspicious, I'll sure give a holler, no kidding."

"Better."

"No problem. And in the meantime, Snort, if you guys find more food than you can handle in there . . . well, you know, I could use some cold beans, a piece of brisket, rib bones, potato salad, just anything you could spare."

Snort laughed. "Hunk talk funnier and funniest. Coyote brothers not leave even one little bite, ho ho."

"Gee, that seems kind of greedy to me."

"What Hunk say?"

"I said, I hope you enjoy your dinner."

He grinned and pointed a paw at me. "And Hunk better not move." And with that, he darted back into the barrel and resumed his digging.

Papers and cans came flying out. I stared up at the stars and tried to forget that I was starving. The minutes crawled by. Ho-hum. This was no fun.

Then, all at once, they stomped out of the barrel. They didn't look real happy. In fact, they looked mad. Snort shot me a glare and snarled, "Not find yummy scraps, only paper and cans."

"I'm sorry, Snort, but is that my fault? I mean, why are you glaring at me? I'm just out here doing my job."

"If brothers not find yummy scraps in next barrel, Hunk job fixing to change, ho ho."

They waded into the next barrel, and soon the air was filled with the sounds of their digging. I waited outside, pondering that last comment of Snort's. It had sounded like a threat to me. "Hunk job fixing to change." Yes, it was a threat, sure 'nuff, and I could only hope . . .

Suddenly the noise stopped and a deep eerie silence moved over us. What was going on? Only seconds before, the brothers had been digging and growling, muttering and laughing, but now . . . now you could hear the tiniest sounds of the night. And fellers, that was a little spooky.

I cocked my head and listened. I heard Snort's voice.

"That you, Rip?"

"Uh-uh."

"Snort see something berry strange in here, like little monster-man with big eyes and long skinny teeth. That not you?"

"Uh-uh."

"Snort think maybe we find garbage monster in here."

"Uh-huh."

"Snort not give a hoot for stay in barrel with garbage monster."

"Uh-uh."

"Snort thinking pretty serious about scram out of here. How about Rip?"

"Uh-huh."

"On count of three, brothers make tracks to canyon."

"Uh!"

"One! Four! Seven!"

I saw two flashes go past and they were out of there. I mean, you'd have thought they'd been shot out of a cannon. All at once *they were gone* and I'd been saved from whatever nastiness they'd been planning for me.

But what was the deal? What had caused them to leave out in such a hurry? I edged my way over to the barrel and peered inside. At first I saw nothing in the gloomy darkness. Then I heard the rattle of some paper and in the darky gloomness I began to see . . .

You won't believe this.

I promise you won't.

It was one of the scariest things I'd seen in my whole career.

It was a Garbage Monster from Outer Space!

CHAPTER TEN

Beware! This Is the Scary Part

Maybe you think there's no such thing as Garbage Monsters from Outer Space, and maybe you think they don't really have big reddish eyes and four white teeth. Well, you think whatever you want. I saw him, and he was a Garbage Monster from Outer Space. No question about it.

And what really chilled me to the bone was that there might have been dozens more of them, hundreds more. For all I knew, the place was crawling with them and I was already surrounded.

Fellers, sometimes I hate to admit that I'm scared. This time I have no problem admitting it. I was scared out of my wits. No wonder Rip and Snort had run off. Heck, I would have run off too,

only ... I didn't. I couldn't. My legs didn't work. They had turned to mush.

I fell down and waited to be eaten by all those red-eyed Garbage Monsters.

It was exactly the kind of response we could have expected from Drover, but not from me. In all my years of Security Work, I had never collapsed in the face of something awful and scary, but this time it happened.

So there I lay on the ground, helpless and pitiful, petrified and paralyzed, and watched the approach of the terrible monster. He was a little guy but had these huge reddish-pink eyes, and we're talking about eyes as big as grapefruit halves, really huge eyes compared to the size of his face.

Did I mention that they were reddish-pink? Maybe so. They were a very spooky color, and they were huge and they had this awful way of *staring at you.* Maybe they were shooting out laser beams or Paralyzer Rays. Yes, that was it. They were shooting out deadly Paralyzer Rays that caused even brave dogs to faint and fall upon the ground.

And those teeth! They were even awfuller than the eyes, scariest things I'd ever seen: skinny white spikes, four of 'em, that resembled . . . I don't know what. The four white spikes on a plastic fork, and they looked very sharp and ready to tear skin from bones and bones from meat and meat from hair and . . .

He spoke.

The monster spoke. I heard his voice, plain as day, a squeaky little voice. I raised my head and swiveled one ear so that I could hear his dreadful message. What would it be, what would he say? Something about "Lowly Earth Dogs, you will now be eaten by the Garbage Monsters from Planet Ozona"?

Anyways, he spoke and I strained to hear every word, and he said . . .

HUH?

I blinked my eyes several times. I took five deep breaths and tried to calm my racing heart.

Whew! You can relax. False alarm. Did you think he was a Garbage Monster from Outer Space? Ha ha. Not me, he didn't fool me for . . . okay, maybe I fell for his trick for a second or two, but it didn't take me long to figure out . . .

It was Eddy the Rac. Can you believe that? Boy, what a relief. Here's the scoop.

See, Eddy was asleep inside that second garbage barrel. All at once he heard noise and woke up and found himself locked inside a barrel with two hungry cannibals. Now, Eddy was a smart little coon, so instead of trying to run or hide, he built himself a disguise with the materials at hand.

He broke off the handle of a plastic fork and placed the bottom half under his upper lip, so that it appeared to be a set of long white fangs. And those eyes, where did he get the eyes? Ha. Two grapefuit halves. (Didn't I say they looked "as big as grapefruits"? I did say that.) He held 'em up to his face, and all at once the little sneak had himself a pretty convincing monster disguise, good enough to send the cannibals fleeing in terror.

It even fooled me for a second or two. When it came to sneaky tricks, Eddy was the champ.

Well, he stepped out of the barrel, dropped his grapefruit eyes, and spit out the fangs. He gave me a grin. "Oh. Hi. How's it going?"

I let the air hiss out of my lungs. "Well, you almost caused me to have a heart attack and a stroke, but otherwise, everything is great."

"Yeah. Coyotes are bad guys. Always hungry. Dumb, too. Fell for those grapefruit eyes. Hee hee."

"Yeah, well, those eyes were pretty convincing, pal, and even some of us who aren't dumb got fooled." I sat down and gave my heart a chance to slow down. "What are you doing over here in the park? Last time I saw you, you were at ranch headquarters."

"Right. I do barrels, move around, stay busy."

"I noticed, and would you like to guess who got blamed for that mess you made at ranch headquarters? ME. I saved your skin and then my skin got caught—and blamed. I'm now living in exile."

"Yeah?"

"Or to put it more accurately, I'm now starving

in exile. I haven't eaten anything but grub worms since I left the ranch in disgrace."

"Bummer. Listen, got a deal."

I stared at him for a long moment. There he was, sitting on his back legs in the moonlight and rolling his busy little hands together. His beady eyes were sparkling with some kind of mischievous light. I had seen all of this before.

"A deal, Eddy? No thanks. I'd just as soon take my chances with cannibals and monsters as do business with you. In the long run, it would be a whole lot safer. In other words, no. No more deals."

"You hungry?"

"No. I'm stuffed." My stomach growled. "Okay, I'm hungry but not desperate or crazy." It growled again. "Okay, I'm starving, but I'd rather starve than . . . what did you have in mind?"

He glanced over both shoulders and motioned me to come closer. I did. He dropped his voice to a whisper. "Listen. Two barrels. One for you, one for me. Fifty-fifty. Quick job, in and out, no heavy lifting. Bingo."

"Eddy, listen to the voice of reason. This is a public park. We could get shot. And besides that, it's wrong. Do you know the difference between right and wrong?"

"Sure. Smell that chicken?"

"No." I sniffed the air. "Yes."

"Does it smell right or wrong?"

"It smells . . . great, if you must know."

"Is great right or wrong?"

"Well . . ."

He threw his hands in the air. "What's great can't be wrong, right? Which barrel you want, left or right?"

"Eddy, I feel that I'm being manipulated."

"Left or right? Need to hurry."

I heaved a sigh. "Eddy, I should know better but . . . okay. Anything that smells as great as that chicken can't possibly be wrong."

He flashed a grin. "See? Bingo. Pick a barrel."

"I pick the one with that chicken smell."

He pointed toward the left barrel. "Canned chicken. Good pick. Smart."

"Thanks, but what is canned chicken?"

"Big can, had a whole chicken inside, lots of gravy on the bottom. Nice pick. You're tough in a deal, got the best end."

"Yeah, well, a guy has to be tough, Eddy, especially when he's doing business with . . ." He walked away and was about to enter his barrel, the one on the right. "Wait a minute, Shorty, and listen to me. I see pink streaks on the horizon. The sun will be up in half an hour, which means that the campers and park rangers will be moving about, which means . . ."

"Right. In and out. Quick job and vanish. Better hurry." He ducked inside the barrel.

"Thirty minutes, pal, and then I'm highballing it back to my ranch. If you're not done, I'll have to leave you."

"Got it."

Well, maybe this wouldn't be so bad. Thirty minutes would be plenty of time for the job. I marched over to the left barrel and crawled inside. I picked up the chicken smell right away. I mean, it was strong and very interesting. This was not your ordinary smell of fried chicken, but a heavier deeper aroma—the aroma of chicken cooked in its own gravy. Wow!

I scratched my way through piles of junk— paper plates and cups, newspapers, soda pop cans—until at last I found the source of the delicious chicken aroma. Eddy had called it right. The fragrant waves were coming from a can, a large can, and I realized right away that most of the delicious gravy was located at the bottom the the can.

Well, that was no big deal. I mean, a lot of your town mutts and ordinary dogs wouldn't have dared to stick their heads into a can, even a large one, because . . . well, fear of tight spots and dark places, I suppose. But that was no impelliment to me. No sir. When I smell chicken gravy, I can't be stopped or discouraged by silly fears. I go right to it and take care of business.

I plunged my nose, face, and entire head into the can, and soon found myself lapping up large quantities of bodaciously good chicken gravy, the best I'd ever eaten. Wonderful stuff. Oh, and amidst the gravy and juice, I also found a few hunks of meat. This was turning out to be a heck of a deal, even better than I had dared to hope.

I mopped it up with my tongue and put a nice little shine on the bottom of the can, and at that point I was ready to . . . well, withdraw my head from the can, but I seemed to be experiencing a little difficulty . . .

Sometimes these cans don't come off as easily as they go on, don't you know, but maybe if I tugged with both paws . . . maybe if I stepped outside the barrel . . .

I stumbled through the garbage mess, slipped on a ketchup bottle, kicked a pickle jar, and finally bulled my way out into the fresh air of morning. It made a lot of noise, but that couldn't be helped.

There. Now all I had to do was . . . if I could just . . .

I pulled. I tugged. I ran backwards and forwards and around in circles. I thrashed my head from side to side and ... BONK ... must have hit a tree or something, and by George, getting my head out from the can was turning out to be ...

"Eddy, we have a little problem here—nothing major, nothing to cause a panic, but I need to borrow your hands for just a few seconds. See, I stuck my head into this stupid can and now ... ha ha . . . I can't seem to get it out, so would you . . ."

I stood still and listened and waited. Nothing.

"Eddy? Listen, pal, this may be a bigger problem than I thought. I know you're busy in there, but I'd be mighty grateful if you'd . . . Eddy! Listen, you little sneak, you got me into this mess and I'm ordering you to come here at once. Do you hear me? Hello? Eddy? Can you hear me?"

I waited and listened. My heart began to stink. Sink, I should say. What I heard was NOT Eddy coming to rescue me from Canned Fate but . . .

. . . the hum of an approaching vehicle.

It stopped. Two men got out. Fellers, I was in deep trouble.

CHAPTER ELEVEN

Arrested by
the Park Police

They began walking in my direction. I could hear the crunch of gravel beneath their feet. Then . . . voices.

Voice One: "Dadgum coons. Look at this mess!"

Voice Two: "They sure wreck a place."

Voice One: "I'd love to catch 'em. Wait a minute. What's that over there?" Silence. Footsteps. My heart was pounding. "It's a dog, and he's got his head stuck in a can!"

Voice Two: "Caught in the act."

Voice One: "Yeah, and do you recognize him? That's Loper's dog. He lives on the next ranch to the east."

Gulp. My fame, it seemed, had caught up with me. I had been caught, exposed, revealed, and identified. Now all that remained . . . oh brother! Maybe, if I was lucky, they would ship me off to . . . somewhere. Devil's Food Island. Prison. The dog pound. I didn't care, as long as they didn't call the ranch and report me to my mister and mattress.

Master and mistress. Whatever. Anything but that. My reputation couldn't stand another Garbage Felony.

Suddenly I heard them laughing. What could this mean? I strained my ear to listen through the can.

Voice One: "Loper and Slim are on the volunteer fire department crew. Every time we get together for a fire meeting, they pull some prank on me. One time they turned a turtle loose under the seat of my pickup. Last Fourth of July they wired up a smoke bomb to the fire truck. I thought I'd burned up the clutch."

Voice Two: "Sounds pretty funny to me."

Voice One: "Uh-huh, and I'm fixing to get paybacks. Can you guess who's going to clean up this garbage mess?"

Voice Two: "Two names come to mind."

Voice One: "I've got 'em this time, Floyd. Old Hank has done me a great service. Let's go back to the office."

I felt a pair of hands on my neck. A moment later the can slipped off my head and I found myself looking into the eyes of Larry Marooney, Park Ranger, and his friend, Floyd Somebody.

I tried to squeeze up a smile, and tapped the last two inches of my tail, as if to say, "I didn't do it, honest. I was just . . . uh . . . walking around with a friend, see, and he . . . he was a coon, a raccoon, and . . . I'm not the kind of dog who tips over garbage barrels, no kidding."

I had expected them to be angry, but they weren't. They seemed very pleasant, to tell you the truth, and they chuckled all the way back to the office. There, Ranger Marooney pulled a cigar from a box on his desk, fired it up, and puffed on it several times. He was still grinning as he looked up Loper's phone number and dialed it.

By the time someone answered, he was looking very serious.

"Hello? Sally May? Morning, ma'am, this is Ranger Marooney over at the park. Uh, we've got a problem over here. We've had a lot of trouble with garbage barrels being overturned. It's been going on for two weeks. Uh-huh, yes ma'am. We thought it was coons, but we've caught the culprit. It's Loper's dog. Yes ma'am, Hank."

Whatever she said was loud. Ranger Marooney

held the phone away from his ear and grinned. He winked at Floyd and went on.

"Now, Sally May, this is pretty serious. We just can't allow stray dogs on the park, and I'm authorized to write up a citation that carries a two-hundred-dollar fine." He flinched and held the phone away from his ear. "Yes ma'am. Now, I'll let y'all off with a warning this time, but I want Loper to come over here and claim his dog and clean up the mess."

He gave Floyd another wink. Then his smile faded. "Oh? Gone to New Mexico? Well, send old Slim over. I guess he's smart enough for this job. He's gone, too? Took some cows to the Beaver City sale? Well, don't you worry about it. Me and Floyd can . . . no, there's no need for you to . . . Sally May, I really didn't mean for you . . . Yes ma'am. We'll be here at the office."

He hung up the phone, stared up at the ceiling, and took three long puffs on the cigar. "Those jugheads. Wouldn't you know they'd both be gone? Loper's wife'll be here in fifteen minutes, and she didn't sound real happy about it."

Floyd got a big laugh out of that. Ranger Marooney didn't, and neither did I.

My heart sank. OH NO, NOT HER! Not Sally May! Anyone but Sally May! Couldn't they just go ahead and shoot me? All at once the thought of being marched in front of a firing squad seemed pretty appealing.

Gulp. I began rehearsing my story.

"Sally May, I know this looks bad, and I understand that you had other things planned for your day . . . uh, besides picking up trash in the . . . uh . . . park. I know you're upset. I know this is a humiliating experience. And I understand that our relationship has been a little . . . well, rocky, you might say . . . that is, we've had a few misunderstandings . . . several misunderstandings and missed opportunities. But I think I can explain everything."

It would never sell. She would never believe that I had been lured into a life of crime by a cheating, scheming, crooked little sneak of a coon.

I was sunk.

The waiting began. What was taking her so long? Well, no doubt she had to round up Little Alfred, put some clothes on Baby Molly, and load them all in the car. That would take some time. But still . . . I hate waiting. It drives me nuts. When a guy is sitting around waiting, all he can do is think.

You know what I was thinking about? My good friend Eddy the Rac. What a scrounge! What a louse! Just walked away and left his friend, his business partner to take the whole rap. Again.

A vehicle was approaching from the east. What? Was she here already? Good grief, what was the rush? I mean, what about rounding up the kids and cleaning their faces? Couldn't we put this off another hour or two? I didn't mind waiting. No kidding. I love to wait, especially when . . .

Gulp.

The door opened. There she was, with Little Alfred at her side and Molly forked on her hip. Her face was . . . uh . . . red, shall we say, dangerously red. Her gaze came straight to me and I wilted. My legs turned to Jell-O. My head sank to the ground. I drew my tail up between my legs and tried to crawl under a chair. That didn't work.

There was only one bright spot in all this. Little Alfred was grinning. That provided some small relief. Alfred was still my pal. He knew I was innocent of all the terrible charges that had been brought against me. Surely Sally May wouldn't strangle me in front of her son.

The Exchange of Prisoners was short and not-so-sweet. Sally May wore a frozen smile throughout the ceremony. She apologized for the actions of her "husband's dog" and assured the park ranger that it wouldn't happen again. Oh, and that her husband would hear all about it when he got home.

Ranger Marooney barked a little laugh at that, but it fell dead in the poisonous atmosphere of the room, I mean, like buckshot falling into a tin plate. He gave her directions to the . . . uh . . . overturned barrels, shall we say, and we left.

Ranger Marooney's parting words were, "Have a good day." He should have kept his mouth shut. That was the wrong thing to say, even I knew that.

We loaded everyone into the pickup. I was a little surprised that she had come in the pickup instead of her car. I knew she didn't enjoy driving the ranch pickups because she hated shifting gears. So why had she . . . oh yes, Loper had driven the car to New Mexico.

When both doors were slammed shut, she shot a glare back toward the office. "I'm going to pick up garbage and he tells me to *have a good day*? That's the stupidest thing I ever heard. If he doesn't have anything intelligent to say, why doesn't he just keep his mouth shut?"

She plunged her left foot down on the clutch pedal. I was down there on the floorboard, trying to hide and be inconspicuous and, you know, just minding my own business. But . . . OOF . . . somehow I managed to . . .

"Hank, will you move? I can't drive this lumber truck with you in the way." I struggled and managed to crawl several inches to the east. She tried again and ... ARG ... "Hank, MOVE! Get out from under my feet! Alfred, get this dog away from me so I can drive."

Alfred called me over to his side of the pickup. I stared at him with puzzled eyes and whapped my tail. I tried to explain that, since Sally May was so mad at me, I felt some need to stay close to her and, you know, try to convince her that I really felt terrible about all this.

And I did, really bad, and lying at her feet seemed the right thing to do. But that was before she started kicking me, and at that point, I ... uh ... moved my business to the other side of the pickup. There I melted into the floormat and beamed Mournful Looks at her.

She stomped the clutch pedal, started the motor, threw the gearshift into first gear, and popped the clutch. Heads snapped back and we lurched away from the parking area. Dust drifted down from the ceiling and two miller moths flew out of the heater vents.

On our way to the, uh, scene of the accident, as you might say, Sally May gripped the wheel with both hands and muttered. It wasn't clear if she was addressing herself or the kids or ... well, me. It was all muttered in a low tone of voice, a kind of hiss. I didn't catch all of it, but I heard enough.

"Tipping over garbage barrels. Eating garbage in the park. They probably think we don't feed you. It'll be all over the neighborhood now that we starve our dogs. You nincompoop, you moron! We spend thirty dollars a month on dog food and this is the thanks we get. You're the . . . sometimes I think . . . oh-h-h!"

Boy, that hurt. But if it made her feel better to say all those things, that was okay. The problem was that it didn't make her feel better. See, she still had to pick up the garbage. That was an experience to remember.

Molly and I stayed in the pickup whilst Sally May and Alfred chased papers. The wind had come up, see, a damp restless wind out of the southeast, and it sure did move those papers around. Alfred made a game of it and seemed to be enjoying himself. Sally May didn't and wasn't.

Boy, was she steamed. Chasing those papers around didn't improve her attitude one bit. She talked to every one of them. I couldn't hear what she said, but she wasn't wishing them happy birthday. Oh, and she had quite a bit to say about the rotting watermelon rinds. They were swarming with flies, don't you see, and Sally May wasn't fond of flies.

Anyways, I felt terrible about it, her having to mingle with the flies and all, whilst I was sitting in the pickup and ... well, watching. Actually, I was doing more than that. I was guarding Baby Molly.

All at once it occurred to me that if Sally May returned to the pickup and found me cleaning up her baby's face, it might ... well ... soften her heart, so to speak. I needed to do something to redeem myself, and fast.

See, by then I had begun to worry that she might ... well ... send me away. That was my worst fear, and fellers, it turned out to be ... you'll see.

CHAPTER TWELVE

Banished from the Ranch? Oh No!

I moved into Molly's lap and began scrubbing her face. See, it was kind of dirty, especially around her mouth. Now, I'd be the last to criticize Sally May or to suggest that she had brought her child out into public with a dirty face, but . . . well, the face was dirty, what can I say?

Hey, I understood. Sally May had been in a hurry. She hadn't taken the time to wash the . . . jelly? You bet it was jelly, homemade grape jelly, which just happened to be a favorite of mine, and by George, the little darlin' had it all around her mouth and even up past her nose. Devotion to duty was tasting better and better and . . . you won't believe this, but she even had some traces of jelly around her left ear! No kidding.

117

So I washed and scrubbed and . . .

"Will you stop licking my baby!"

Huh? Sure, but she had . . . that is, I thought . . .

"Alfred, put that dog in the back of the pickup and you ride with him."

Okay, fine. Maybe she wanted her kids running around in public with jelly and cracker crumbs and mud and dirt all over their faces. Maybe she didn't care what the neighbors might think, and if she wanted everyone thinking that she raised filthy children, that was okay with me.

Boy, once you get on the wrong side of Sally May, it's hard to get off the list.

We rode in the back, Alfred and I. Perhaps Sally May had thought this was punishment. It wasn't. I could hardly disguise my relief at being away from her frigid glares and cutting words. See, Alfred and I were special pals. He seemed to understand the burdens and cares of being a dog. We sat together on the spare tire, he with his arm around my neck.

"Welp," he said when we got under way, "I guess you got in twouble again, Hankie."

I nodded and shrugged. What could I say? I studied his face and decided that it was time to, uh, probe for some classified information, so to speak.

"Say, pardner, what do you suppose your ma has in mind for me? I mean, she seems to be pretty sore." His gaze moved away. "Is it bad? Come on, son, you can tell me. We've been through a lot together. We're special pals, right?"

He nodded and pressed his lips together. "Mom says we have to . . . give you away."

Give me away! Those words echoed through the inner chambers of my mind. It sent little needles of electricity down my spine.

We stared into each other's eyes for a long time. So this was the way it would end—not with a bang, not with loud music or drumrolls, but with me and my little pal saying good-bye in the back of the pickup. I swallowed a lump in my throat.

"Well, gee, I don't know what to say. Just . . . so long, I guess, and thanks for all the good times."

He nodded and bit his lip. "Maybe you should wun off and hide. I'd find you and we could pway."

I smiled at that. "Nah, that wouldn't work. I'm just not a runaway kind of dog. Cowdogs don't run from trouble. We live by the law, and when we break the law, we stick around and take the consequences. I messed up pretty severely and I'll take what comes."

"I don't want to give you away."

"Well, I'm not too crazy about that myself, kiddo, but you know what? Miracles sometimes happen. It's never over until the fat lady eats her dessert."

"What does that mean?"

"It means . . . it means that we'll take justice as it comes and then hope for the best."

His little eyes narrowed. "I'll sneak out tonight and we'll wun away."

"Nah. That wouldn't last two hours. You'd get cold and hungry and you'd be ready to go back to your ma."

He pooched out his lips. "I'm mad at my mom."

"Oh, don't be too hard on her. She's a fine lady . . . a little strange sometimes, but she's got a big job, taking care of a house and two kids. And you know what? If I'd been your ma and some guy had called me up . . . well, listen to this."

See, I had a little song in mind, and I sang it for him.

If I'd Been Your Ma

If I'd been your ma and she'd been me,
I'd put me in jail and throw away the key.
She's a little bit strange but a fine old gal,
And she takes good care of my favorite pal.

Now, put yourself in your momma's shoes,
When the telephone rings and she gets the
    news

That her husband's dog's running through
    the park
On a rip, on a tear, on a midnight lark,

If I'd been your ma, and she'd been me,
I'd put me in jail and throw away the key.
She's a little bit strange but a fine old gal,
And she takes good care of my favorite pal.

Trash cans crash, making papers fly,
And the park ranger calls . . . you can under-
    stand why
It would make her mad and offend her pride.
Picking garbage up is undignified.

If I'd been your ma and she'd been me,
I'd put me in jail and throw away the key.
She's a little bit strange but a fine old gal,
And she takes good care of my favorite pal.

So let's don't judge what your parents do,
They work real hard to provide for you.
I shoulda brought my fun to a screeching halt.
If I get shipped off, it's my own derned fault.

If I'd been your ma and she'd been me,
I'd put me in jail and throw away the key.

She's a little bit strange but a fine old gal,
And she takes good care of my favorite pal.

When I'd finished the song, I looked at the boy. "So there it is, son. Don't get mad at your mother and don't blame her for whatever happens in this deal. What I did was wrong. I knew it was wrong and I did it anyway. A guy has to pay for his bad habits."

We pulled into headquarters and parked behind the house. Sally May climbed out of the pickup and pulled Molly out. She slammed the door and muttered something about "nasty ranch pickups." I didn't catch all of it.

Then her eyes came up and found us in the back of the pickup. There we were, Two Pals for Life, sitting together on the spare tire, with Little Alfred hugging my neck and pressing his face against my ear. I beamed her Most Sincere and Woeful Looks of Remorse, and switched my tail section over to Slow Sweeps.

Her eyes went from one of us to the other. She cocked her head to the side and compressed her lips. "Alfred, don't make this harder than it needs to be. I've already made my decision. Hank has to go."

"But Mom, Hankie and I have a deal."

Her left eyebrow twitched. "You have . . . a deal?"

"Uh-huh. See, we've talked it ovoo and Hankie's vewy sad for what he did."

We held our breaths and waited to see what she would say. "You and Hank *talked* it *over*?"

"Uh-huh, we did. And Hankie's vewy sad."

A smile twitched at her mouth. "What are you two cooking up? Whatever it is, the answer is NO."

"Hewe's the deal, Mom. If you'll wet Hankie stay, we're boff gonna be good. I'm gonna make my bed evwee day and bwush my teeff and pick up my socks. And Hankie's gonna give up twash, aren't you, Hankie?"

I gave my tail five hard whaps on the spare tire and held my head at an angle that showed . . . well, honesty, sincerity, and the very purest of intentions.

A chirp of laughter flew out of her mouth. "That's the craziest thing I ever heard. You two scamps promising to be good?" Her laughter grew louder and wilder. Then it stopped and she forked us with her eyes. "No. A skunk will always be a skunk. A leopard can't change his spots. Hank loves garbage barrels and he needs to find another home."

Well, that was the end of it. The boy had tried. But then he threw his arms around my neck and began crying.

"Mom, Hankie's my best fwind in the whole world. I wuv him. If you send him away, you have to send me away too."

Her jaw dropped every so slightly. She stared at us. Then her eyes rolled back in her head. "I do not believe this. My son loves . . . oh, brother! This wasn't covered in Dr. Dobson's book." She walked a few steps away and resettled baby Molly on her hip. When she turned back to us, her expression was hard, firm, unforgiving, and cold. It looked bad. "All right, Alfred. I can't be the wicked witch forever. You two have worn me down."

"And Hankie can stay?"

She heaved a sigh. "I don't know who would take him anyway. I sure wouldn't give him to a friend. I'll probably regret this, but . . . all right, he can stay *this one last time.*"

"Yippee!"

By George, we'd done it!

"BUT . . ." She aimed a finger at the two of us, which cut short our little celebration. "But you'd better remember all those things you promised, young man, and you'd better tell your friend Hank to stay home, stay away from the park, stay out of garbage barrels, out of my yard, out of my flower beds—and out of sight for about two weeks." Her gaze swung around and pierced me. "Mister McNasty, the less we see of each other, the better it'll be—especially for you."

Oh yes ma'am, no problem. Right then and there, in front of Sally May and everybody, I took a Solemn Oath to be a perfect and well-behaved dog, and I mean forever and ever.

She wouldn't even know I was on the ranch. No more barking at night for me, no more beating up her stupid . . . uh . . . no more bickering with her Precious Kitty . . . Pete, that is. And above all, no more garbage picking in the park with Eddy the Rac.

No sir, that was all behind me. I was a new dog. Honest.

Alfred gave me one last hug and jumped down to the ground. "Come on, Hankie, wet's go pway."

We fled the scene, so to speak, and left Sally May . . . well, still muttering and shaking her head—although I did notice that she cracked one little smile.

And that's about it. Little Alfred had saved me from being shipped off and I was back on my ranch again, only now I was a much wiser dog, a reformed dog, a dog who would be forever dedicated to being a Model of Good Behavior.

Maybe you're suprised. Maybe you thought

I went straight to Pete and chased him up a tree and gave him the thrashing he so richly deserved. Nope. That stuff was all behind me. I waited two whole days to beat the snot out of him and run him up a tree, and Sally May never even suspected it.

Heh, heh.

Case closed.

Have you read all of Hank's adventures?

Join Hank the Cowdog's Security Force

Are you a big Hank the Cowdog fan? Then you'll want to join Hank's Security Force. Here is some of the neat stuff you will receive:

Welcome Package
- A Hank paperback embossed with Hank's top secret seal
- Free Hank bookmarks

Eight issues of *The Hank Times* with
- Stories about Hank and his friends
- Lots of great games and puzzles
- Special previews of future books
- Fun contests

More Security Force Benefits
- Special discounts on Hank books and audiotapes
- An original Hank poster (19" x 25") absolutely free

Total value of the Welcome Package and *The Hank Times* is $23.95. However, your two-year membership is **only $8.95** plus $3.00 for shipping and handling.

☐ Yes I want to join Hank's Security Force. Enclosed is $11.95 ($8.95 + $3.00 for shipping and handling) for my **two-year membership**. [Make check payable to Maverick Books.]

Which book would you like to receive in your Welcome Package? Choose from books 1–30.

(#   )   (#   )

FIRST CHOICE   SECOND CHOICE

BOY or GIRL

YOUR NAME   (CIRCLE ONE)

MAILING ADDRESS

CITY   STATE   ZIP

TELEPHONE   BIRTH DATE

E-MAIL

Are you a ☐ Teacher or ☐ Librarian?

Send check or money order for $11.95 to:

Hank's Security Force
Maverick Books
PO Box 549
Perryton, Texas 79070

DO NOT SEND CASH. NO CREDIT CARDS ACCEPTED.
Allow 4–6 weeks for delivery.

The Hank the Cowdog Security Force, the Welcome Package, and The Hank Times are the sole responsibility of Maverick Books. They are not organized, sponsored, or endorsed by Penguin Putnam Inc., Puffin Books, Viking Children's Books, or their subsidiaries or affiliates.